Contents

Sponsored by Demons
The Art of Jeanette Winterson

Scholars' Press

879 874 7703

Sponsored by Demons: The Art of Jeanette Winterson

Copyright © the authors and Scholars' Press 1999

First edition, ISBN 87 - 987477 - 0 - 3

Cover illustration by Louise Holmegaard Madsen

Printed on recycled paper by Blommenslyst Bogtrykkeri
Odense, Denmark

Scholars' Press
www.scholars.dk

Abbreviations and Editions Used in this Book

Oranges *Oranges Are Not the Only Fruit.* (1st ed. 1985). London: Vintage, 1990.

Boating *Boating for Beginners.* (1st ed. 1985). London: Minerva, 1990.

The Passion *The Passion.* (1st ed. 1987). London: Vintage, 1996.

Sexing *Sexing the Cherry.* (1st ed. 1989). London: Vintage, 1990.

Written *Written on the Body.* (1st ed. 1992). London: Vintage, 1996.

ArtOb *Art Objects.* (1st ed. 1995). London: Vintage, 1996.

GutS *Gut Symmetries.* London: Granta, 1997.

World *The World and Other Places.* London: Jonathon Cape, 1998.

Editors' Preface

This collection of essays is the collaborative effort of a group of students and teachers affiliated with the University of Southern Denmark - Odense and the University of Copenhagen who are fascinated by the art of Jeanette Winterson. Courses on Winterson and discussions about her work, both in and out of the classroom, have made us eager to read her writing so as to illuminate aspects of her art that have been overshadowed by critical focus on feminist and lesbian issues.

What has emerged is a collection of readings which offers variations on other themes, many of them recurring throughout our essays, as they do in Winterson's oeuvre: love, subjectivity, and the problems of giving voice to singular experience through language; postmodern and premodern aspects of Winterson's art; the role of the feminine for notions of identity; Winterson's place within, and stance toward, tradition; and her imaginative visions of worlds and beings which attest to the power of the creative word to test— and expand—the reader's conceptions of what is real, what is possible, and what is desirable.

A brief note on the first part of the title of this collection might be pertinent: the demonic sponsorship is taken from *Boating for Beginners*, a work of which Winterson is not particularly proud, but which is, like other experimental fragments, eloquent of choices wanting to be made. Here, an orange demon interrupts a mysterious dream in which the protagonist finds an eagle bursting out of her stomach. The demon's question foregrounds already strong intertextual links to a series of poetic quests all seeking to define a poet's relation to tradition: "A word from your sponsors. Did you grow out of the eagle or did the eagle grow out of you?" Gloria doesn't know the answer. Winterson does. She knows that her texts—prophetic, she hopes, enunciations of an ambitious, if slightly quixotic, Gloria Munde—are both before and after *her* sponsors, existing with them in the same realm of daemonic inspiration—that of the imaginary—where works old and new mix with each other, waiting once again to be born of eagles erupting out of poets.

The present text, too, has come into being with the help of a number of "sponsors". We would like to express our thanks to Louise Holmegaard Madsen for letting us use her beautiful work for our cover image; to Lennart Maagaard for his help in making the text print-ready; to the English Department at the University of Southern Denmark – Odense for their financial assistance; to Benny Petersen for good counsel on matters of printing; to Dexel A/S for their help in putting us in print; and to the many students who have participated in courses on Jeanette Winterson and Angela Carter and influenced and inspired our readings.

Listening for the Author's Voice:
"Un-Sexing" the Wintersonian Oeuvre
by Louise Horskjær Humphries

When asked about her role as a spokesperson for women and lesbians in a recent interview—does she feel a pressure from such quarters?—Jeanette Winterson replied:

> Oh, yes! But it would be a very bad thing indeed if I were to do that.... I have no objection to all of this stuff being pumped out; there really is a place for it. But I don't want to do it. I don't want to be a political writer, or a writer whose concern is sexual politics.[1]

None the less, these are precisely the terms in which Winterson repeatedly is identified as a writer. This article arises, in part at least, from a regret that so much academic criticism approaches Winterson's oeuvre as strictly lesbian literature; that is, sees Winterson as a political riter whose principal merit is her promotion of the lesbian-feminist cause. Such frequent "sexing" of Winterson's writing— often with a reference to her real-life sexual preference—also meets resistance from the writer herself: "[a]rt is difference", she says, but "not necessarily sexual difference" (*Art Objects,* p. 105); reading should be sexy rather than sexed. Hence, my reason for choosing to play on the word "sexing" in my title—a word so often used (abused it seems) in the titles of critical essays—is simultaneously to evoke

[1] Jeanette Winterson in interview with Audrey Bilger, "The Art of Fiction CL", *The Paris Review*, 145 (1997 – 98), p. 105.

such strategies and suggest their potential undoing.

Certainly, lesbian-feminist criticism[2] cannot be rejected on the grounds that it is not talented; in fact, much of it is highly perceptive and clever. I do not mean to suggest that there is not a space for it either, but contest that if Winterson at some level invites ideological criticism, this specific interpretive key encourages an approach which is at best partial and always reductive. As James Held rightly points out, none of Winterson's novels "are lesbian/feminist manifestos or ... offer a coherent political program";[3] in fact, her engagement with lesbian/feminst theory "can best be described as visionary pragmatism" (Held, p. 201)[4] —a point which seems to find corroboration from Winterson's observation on all "conceptual frameworks" available to human beings "which are all and always provisional" (*Gut Symmetries*, p. 168).

The following, then, offers a critique of the tendency to see lesbianism as centred in Winterson's writing, and to assess its merits according to how well it complies with lesbian-feminist (literary) theory. This critique will take the form of a discussion of specific examples of Winterson criticism with a special focus on *Oranges Are Not the Only Fruit* and *Written on the Body,* as these two in particular seem to be at either end of a lesbian-feminist critical barometre. What I hope to suggest, then, is not to what extent lesbian-feminist theory, generally speaking, holds value, but rather how the approach—partly by force of its sheer dominance—actually results in a depreciation of the "vastness" of Winterson's fictional universe. However, even as it is my contention that it is the prerogative of any reader/critic to do with a text what he or she wants—texts are unfixed and indeterminate and posit an infinite number of readings—I still find it reasonable to ask what the "political activism" of much of this critical writing has to do with

---

[2] Winterson is, in fact, variously placed in contexts of "queer", "radical lesbian", and "lesbian-feminist" politics. These are all terms under fierce debate, but one crucial distinction between "queer" theory and "lesbian-feminist" theory would seem to be that where the former emphasizes "difference", the latter emphasizes "sameness". At the same time that I do not wish to ignore the diversity of this field of theory, inevitably reflected in Winterson criticism, I need a term which is at once sufficiently inclusive and exclusive to enable me to use it as an overall term. Partly by virtue of its conjunction, "lesbian-feminist" indicates an area of shared concerns and assumptions between lesbians and feminists—a resistance to patriarchy and sexism, and the belief that literature is the site for voicing such resistance, but also differences within this sameness—lesbians also struggle against heterosexism. Hence, when I speak of the lesbian-feminist approach, I do not refer to a stable category of criticism (nor a stable category of identity behind it), but simply use it as a recognizable adjective for the kind of political discourse with which I am presently concerned.

[3] James Held, *A Dream of Essence: Permutations of the Self in Contemporary Fiction* (Ph.D. dissertation, Temple University, 1995), p. 199.

[4] For all her "postmodern" concerns, her intellectual and clever analyses of the nature of humans, art, time, etc., Winterson never loses sight of "ordinary experience". The link between language and life is never allowed to be severed. In this sense, the question reiterated by Handel in *Art & Lies*— "[h]ow shall I live?" (p. 25)—is fundamental to all her novels.

literary criticism. In his introduction to *Lesbian and Bisexual Women Writers*, Harold Bloom voices a valuable concern with feminist literary criticism. Posing the questions "is there really an essential difference between men's and women's writing?", and "if there is, do we need different aesthetical standards for judging it?", Bloom argues that, while he has not got the answers to such questions, "[t]he consequences of making gender a criterion for aesthetic choice must finally destroy all serious study of imaginative literature as such".[5] For Bloom, then, there is a clear distinction between studying gender and studying art; to sex art is, in a manner of speaking, precisely to deny art its "artness":

> Gender studies are precisely that: they study gender, and not aesthetic value. If your priorities are historical, social, political and ideological, then gender studies clearly are more than justified. Yet that is a very different matter from the now vexed issue of aesthetic value (Bloom, p. xiii).

Whether one agrees with Bloom that such a distinction can be upheld or not,[6] feminist criticism certainly rejects Literature as a special kind of discourse; a status Winterson most definitely allows it.[7]

> I was in a bookshop recently when a young woman approached me. She told me she was writing an essay on my work and that of Radclyffe Hall. Could I help ? 'Yes,' I said. 'Our work has nothing in common.' 'I thought you were a lesbian.'[sic] she said (*ArtOb*, p. 103).
> I was in a bookshop recently and a young man came up to me and said 'Is Sexing the Cherry a reading of Four Quartets?' 'Yes' I said, and he kissed me (*ArtOb*, p. 118).

---

[5] Harold Bloom, *Lesbian and Bisexual Women Writers* (Philadelphia: Chelsea House Publishers, 1997), p. xii.

[6] Lidia Curti, for one, does not. "One of the specific contributions of feminism is precisely the overcoming of such dichotomies [form and content, politics and art]". Lidia Curti, *Female Stories, Female Bodies: Narrative, Identity and Representation.* (London: Macmillan, 1998), p. 87. In her study, Curti identifies "hybridity" as a concept central to contemporary feminist writing—fiction as well as theory—"liminal styles of writing inbetween the poetical and the political registre" (p. xi).

[7] Speaking of the relationship between precisely feminism and postmodernism Linda Hutcheon notes a shared deconstructive impulse: "[t]hey all ... challenge what we consider to be literature (or rather, Literature)". Linda Hutcheon, *The Politics of Postmodernism* (London and New York: Routledge, 1989), p. 23. Winterson, however, does not seem to share contemporary distrust of all "master narratives"; in fact, she seems in her view of art (or Art) closer to modernism than postmodernism. See, for example the epigraph to *Art & Lies*. See also Cindie Aaen Maagaard, "The Word Embodied in *Art & Lies*", in this volume.

from 'Listening for the Author's Voice:
"Un-Sexing" the Wintersonian Oeuvre' In:
Sponsored by Demons: The Art of Jeanette Winterson.
Eds. Bengtson et al. 1999. Odense. Scholar's Press.

Jeanette Winterson obviously regrets a foregrounding of her sexuality in connection with a discussion of her writing; she is, as she says, "a writer who happens to love women ... not a lesbian who happens to write" (*ArtOb,* p. 104). Winterson's anecdotes clearly serve as a critique of a tendency to confuse the autobiography of a writer with her writing, at the same time that they suggest where in literary tradition she would like to see herself, but also how she sees herself as an avid reader—and ultimately re-writer—of that tradition. To this extent the anecdotes at once provide a clue to what kind of reader/critic Winterson respects—someone who pays attention to the language as well as the literary tradition which are always echoed in her writing, and what kind of reader/critic she disrespects—someone who confuses the writer's biography with her work of art.

Indeed, throughout Winterson's "aesthetic credo", *Art Objects*, she argues in favour of the transpersonality of true Art. Like her much-admired precursor, T.S. Eliot, she firmly believes that, for the artist, autobiography must be translated into writing in which it is transfigured into unrecognizability.[8] The writer, if a good one, is only present in her art as language, as words on the page, and there is no way of translating these back into autobiography. Thus, when she says in the introduction to *Oranges Are Not the Only Fruit* that it both is and is not autobiography,[9] Winterson is not only rejecting the distinction between autobiography (traditionally aligned with truth) and fiction (lie), she is also acknowledging—celebrating even—the transformative power of art. Art springs from life, but transcends it; rather than being a mirror of life it is a transformation of it. In this way "transpersonal" also comes to imply some kind of "universality" which means that art will reach across boundaries of time, class, gender, and sexuality. "Literature is not a lecture delivered to a special interest group, it is a force that unites its audience", Winterson states explicitly in *Art Objects* (p. 106).

While I do not mean to suggest that one needs to consult Winterson on how to read her, or uncritically accept her statements about her own writing, I believe that she is right when she rejects lesbianism as the key to her fiction. Interestingly, many of the critics who approach Winterson from this angle see evidence of a clear distinction in her oeuvre. Thus, while *Oranges* is generally hailed as "one of those success stories of which feminists feel proud",[10] many lesbian-feminist critics have felt that Winterson in her subsequent

---

[8] Significantly, Winterson's books are full of the alchemical image. "'*Tertium non data':* the third element is not given. That is, the transformation from one element to another ... is a process that cannot be documented. It is fully mysterious" (*Sexing the Cherry,* p. 131). See also *Gut Symmetries,* pp. 137 - 38, and *Art & Lies,* p. 6.

[9] p. xiv. The introduction was added to the Vintage edition in 1991, and appears in all subsequent editions.

novels has failed the lesbian cause as she has apparently withdrawn from material politics to a realm of the imaginary and fantastic. Lynne Pearce sums up the common charges, and reveals that particularly the narrator—gender unidentified—in *Written on the Body* has been the course of much upset from the feminist literary establishment: "the refusal to 'name'" the narrator has been considered nothing less than "a serious political betrayal".[11] *Written*, however, is not the only one of Winterson's texts which has been faulted with representing love as a "universal" emotion which may ultimately transcend all differences. In both *The Passion* and *Sexing the Cherry* "the inclusion of a broad spectrum of characters of different gender and sexual preferences" (Pearce, p. 174) has been seen to result in a "normalization" rather than a politicization of homosexuality. Villanelle's love for the "Queen of Spades" is neither presented as a political choice, nor as essentially different from Henri's love (unrequited) for Villanelle. Hence, "Villanelle's love affair cannot be said to be lesbian in any real political sense" (Pearce, p. 174). While Pearce disagrees with such charges and sets out to defend Winterson, I actually find much truth in them. What particularly worries me, however, is the fact that Winterson's writing is weighed against some assumptions about what lesbian literature should and should not do, and subsequently found too light.

It would seem from the ongoing debate that one of the more stable criteria

---

[10] Hilary Hinds, "*Oranges Are Not the Only Fruit*: Reaching Audiences Other Lesbian Texts Cannot Reach", in *The New Lesbian Criticism: Literary and Cultural Readings*, ed. Sally Munt (Hempel Hampstead: Harvester Wheatsheaf, 1992), p. 153. Hilary Hinds, in her analysis of the reception of *Oranges*, suggests that its popularity with non-lesbian readers was conditioned partly by the fact that it "was read in a cultural context where high-cultural 'art' had been established as having a meaning separable from questions of politics, sexual and otherwise" (Hinds, p. 159) which made a "universal" reading possible. Thus, she assumes that lesbianism is a centre in the text, which non-lesbian readers, due to various circumstances, may have been able to ignore, but which is nevertheless "really" there. To argue that only lesbian readers read Winterson for what she really is, not only assumes that all lesbians read alike, but also suggests a kind of cultural separatism against which Winterson herself warns in *Art Objects* (p. 110).

[11] Lynne Pearce, *Reading Dialogics* (London: Edward Arnold, 1994), p. 174. In another article Pearce identifies in Winterson's texts "an ambivalence that centres on a tension between the perception of romantic love as a non-gendered, a-historic, a-cultural 'universal', and as an 'ideology' which the specificities of gender and sexual orientation constantly challenge". Lynne Pearce, "Written on Tablets of Stone?: Roland Barthes, Jeanette Winterson and the Discourse of Romantic Love", in *Volcanoes and Pearl Divers: Essays in Lesbian Feminist Studies,* ed. S. Raitt (London: Onlywoman Press, 1995), p. 148. This ambivalence, Pearce argues, makes it possible for the heterosexual reader to read the same-sex love as merely incidental, which helps to account for Winterson's general popularity. "Yet to read the novels in this way is ... to be blind to the angst at their (romantic) heart" (p. 148), Pearce claims and sets out to prove how Winterson's novels finally contest the "universals" of Roland Barthes' *A Lover's Discourse*, against which she reads Winterson. Similarly to Hinds, then (see above), Pearce argues in favour of "particular" readings, and although she has many interesting points, I disagree with this conclusion.

for lesbian fiction is lesbianism in the sense of a political choice, that is, as a means for criticizing and subverting patriarchal and heterosexual discourse.[12] This is confirmed by Lisa Moore in an article concerned with the way in which Winterson's novels at once invoke and deviate from both postmodern and lesbian theories and narrative conventions. Winterson's fiction, she argues, rejects a central assumption of lesbian theory: the "lesbian" as inherently radical and subversive, occupying a marginal space outside of the "symbolic order" from which she may challenge heterosexual culture. For Winterson such a distinction does not hold; "she represents lesbianism simply as central, rather than 'opposed' to anything. There is very little representation of homophobia, very little recognizably 'political' in her fiction"[13]—what little there is, Moore locates in *Oranges*. Thus, at the same time that she consolidates a division in the Wintersonian oeuvre, Moore identifies the distinguishing mark of Winterson's later fiction as a "decisive distance from contemporary sexual politics" (Moore, p. 113).

It is *Oranges,* then—arguably Winterson's most realistic novel, and, in the eyes of many critics, also an unmistakably political work[14]—which has most unambiguously been identified as one of "the few canonical texts which are central to the fledgling lesbian literary tradition".[15] However, I disagree with the critics who see *Oranges* in terms of a distinct difference of concern from the rest of her oeuvre, and with the readings of the novel on which such a view is founded.

---

[12] Again, this is not an undisputed area. Critics are far from in agreement as to what the criteria for a definition of lesbian-feminist fiction should be: written *by*?, written *for*?, or written *about* lesbians? Paulina Palmer rejects all three, but says specifically about the last criteria that it does not work because "lesbian feminist perspectives are identifiable as much by a political critique of heterosexuality and male power, as by an analysis of love between women". Paulina Palmer, "Contemporary Lesbian Feminist Fiction: Texts for Everywoman", in *Plotting Change: Contemporary Women's Fiction*, ed. Linda Anderson (London: Edward Arnold, 1990), p. 45. A novel, then, can be "lesbian" without explicitly dealing with lesbian erotics. Interestingly, Lillian Faderman suggests that the opposite can be true too, when she asks if it is reasonable to exclude a work like *Oranges* from the lesbian canon. While lesbianism is neither at the centre of that story, nor represented as a political choice—Jeanette just happens to be lesbian—the novel, she argues, is clearly lesbian. Lillian Faderman, "What Is Lesbian Literature? Forming a Historical Canon", in *Professions of Desire: Lesbian and Gay Studies in Literature,* eds. George E. Haggerty and Bonnie Zimmerman (New York: Modern Language Association of America, 1995), p. 53.

[13] Lisa Moore, "Teledildonics: Virtual Lesbians in the Fiction of Jeanette Winterson", in *Sexy Bodies: The Strange Carnalities of Feminism*, eds. Elizabeth Groz and Elspeth Probyn (London: Routledge, 1995), p. 108.

[14] For some (especially early) feminists the realistic mode would seem to offer the best possibilities for furthering political ends. They have consequently been troubled by an apparent abandonment of the "real" in much contemporary feminist writing. As a fictional autobiography, *Oranges*, of course, suggests that such distinctions between "what is real" and "what is not" simply does not hold— "there's only art and lies" (*A&L,* p. 69).

[15] Sally Munt, Introduction to *The New Lesbian Criticism: Literary and Cultural Readings*, ed. Sally Munt (Hempel Hampstead: Harvester Wheatsheaf, 1992), p. xx.

In all of her novels, Winterson explores and develops ideas about art, love, and subjectivity, and, not least, the ways in which they intersect with and illuminate each other. Even as there is a shift in focus from speculation as to what creates a person to a concern with what constitutes one, the quest motif continually occupies centre-ground.[16] In this quest for self,[17] which is simultaneously a quest for language, love, as the highest possible human energy, is the one force capable of gathering some kind of essence. "What has defined me at the clearest point of my outspread life has been my love for you.... A fix in the flux" (*GutS*, pp. 206 - 7).

Admittedly, *Oranges* is at some level specifically about lesbian desire in a heterosexually dominated culture—here represented by the Church—and as such offers a challenge to patriarchal and heterosexist discourse. However, more than that, it is about the creation of a person (artist-prophet) and love's role as a kind of catalyst in the quest for identity. In the process of finding a self, Jeanette has to learn a very important lesson about the multiplicity of truth: "no emotion is the final one" (*Oranges,* p. 48). Surprisingly, Laura Doan, in fact, argues that Winterson's first novel fails to live up to "the political agenda" of the lesbian writer which is "to explode the binary".[18] "Winterson remains (albeit unwittingly) in the realm of parody, of imitation, in the unproblematic reversal of binary terms— a strategy that privileges the status of the lesbian over that of the heterosexual but doesn't facilitate an ongoing critique" (Doan, p. 146). Thus, at the same time that Doan defines a political goal for the lesbian-feminist writer—"strategies ... which ... will neutralize heteropatriarchal authority and begin to map an alternative social order, one that positions the lesbian at the center" (Doan, p. 145)—she measures *Oranges* against it, and determines that it fails to meet this requirement. But can *Oranges* seriously be faulted for not complying with a lesbian political agenda, and is Winterson really engaged in a simple reversal of binaries? Rightly, Jeanette plays with the Church's notions of what is natural and unnatural, but rather than privileging lesbianism (good and natural) over heterosexuality (evil and unnatural), she reveals such notions to be constructs—relative rather than absolute—which opens up the possibility of a complete re-thinking of things. Her break with the Church is a break with a world of black and white in which

---

[16] As stated by Jordan in *Sexing* (pp. 102 - 3), humans, unlike God, are incomplete in themselves, and therefore conditioned to a perpetual search for wholeness of some kind. (See also *Gut Symmetries,* pp. 4 - 5).The outward search for an other, however, usually turns out to be an inward search for self; that is, the quest for passion, in fact, leads you "home", to find yourself in the other.

[17] Selves rather, as we are not only our realized selves, but also our potentially realized identities; the journeys taken as well as those not taken. In all of Winterson's novels identity is suggested as multiple and fluid, a cluster of possibilities, a state of fluxes. See, for example, *Oranges,* p. 164, and *Sexing,* pp. 9 - 10, p. 80, and p. 90.

[18] Laura Doan, "Jeanette Winterson's Sexing the Postmodern", in *The Lesbian Postmodern* (New York: Columbia UP, 1994), p. 147.

homosexuality can only be natural or unnatural, good or evil, and in which perfection is a matter of "flawlessness" rather than balance. It seems, then, that *Oranges* works on a different level, that it is simply not, as Doan wants it to be, directly or "actively" political.[19]

Love, then, indirectly teaches Jeanette that truth is always provisional and in this sense triggers her decision to leave the Church. It is, however, a very specific moment in the novel which brings about her rebellion.[20] The Church explains lesbianism in terms of inversion. Having been granted the power to preach in church, Jeanette has, in fact, usurped male power—"the message belonged to the men" (*Oranges,* p. 131). The fact that she has been given entrance into a male domain in this way has caused her to believe she must "ape" men sexually as well. "So there I was, my success in the pulpit being the reason for my downfall. The devil had attacked me at my weakest point: my inability to realize the limitations of my sex" (p. 132). Jeanette ultimately breaks with the Church because the Word is taken from her, because she is silenced on the grounds of being a woman. While it is difficult to ignore the feminist (political) implications of this moment, I would still argue that it is, if not superseded by, then at least only a part of, a broader epistemological concern with the role of language in the constitution of a person, or, more specifically, of an artist.

Jeanette "blows her trumpet" and refuses to be silenced by patriarchal, heterosexist discourse. Thus, in *Oranges* she tells the story of how she re-claimed the Word for herself and asserted her right to appropriate it for her own purposes; that is, it traces the journey—physical as well as spiritual—of how she became a prophet-artist, her own storyteller.[21] In this way *Oranges* aligns itself with a long

---

[19] In her study of the politics of representation Linda Hutcheon makes a distinction between, on the one hand, the implicitly political (postmodernism)—that is, political in the sense that all forms of representation are inevitably never disinterested, and, on the other, the explicitly or actively political (feminism). Unlike feminism, "the postmodern has no effective theory of agency that enables a move into political *action* (Hutcheon, p. 3, original emphasis). Hutcheon's postmodernism is a mode of "complicitous critique", at once inscribed in and subversive of the ideologies it lays bare, and in this double encoding it remains politically ambiguous (p.168). This helps explain why feminists (and lesbians) traditionally have regarded the postmodern mode with some scepticism, and—in Hutcheon's view—why the two can never be conflated. Doan directly engages in a critique of Hutcheon's theory and suggests that "Winterson pursues her political agenda through a postmodern writing practice" (Doan, p. 139). *Sexing the Cherry* is, however, her only really successful attempt at "sexing" the postmodern. Heidi Hansson in a brilliant study on postmodern romances—a framework in which she reads many of Winterson's novels—also evokes Hutcheon and makes a distinction similar to hers. Feminism, she argues, functions as a cultural intertext in postmodern romances, "but since they are not organised through a binary paradigm—male versus female—it becomes difficult to interpret them in political terms". Winterson's works are "politically aware, although not politically committed". Heidi Hansson, *Romance Revisited: Postmodern Romances and the Tradition* (Umeå University, 1998), p. 64.

[20] Thank you to Marianne Børch for pointing this out to me.

10

tradition of "portrait of the artist" autobiographies, from Dante to Joyce. Lyn Pykett says about *Oranges* that "like Joyce's *bildungsroman* it is less a form of self-expression and self-representation than self-invention.... not simply the story of the making of the artist ... but it is also, in its form, an embodiment of that artist's aesthetic".[22] Pykett refers to Winterson's unfaltering belief in the artist's right to rewrite old stories; indeed, her duty always to create something genuinely new. To be a succesful experimental writer one must, in fact, be equally committed to tradition and innovation (T.S. Eliot again). Winterson explicitly stresses the creative process as a two-fold one: "the calling of the artist, in any medium, is to make it new. I do not mean that in the new work the past is repudiated; quite the opposite, the past is reclaimed" (*ArtOb*, p. 129). Art, then, not only springs from experience, it also springs from other art; another reason why one should never confuse the author's biography with her texts. As Winterson appropriates both generic categories and specific texts—(medieval) romance, fairy tale, the Bible, (canonized) literary fathers and mothers alike—for her own writing, her novels truly qualify as "intertextual palimpsests" (Curti, p. 40). To read *Oranges* as a lesbian "coming-out" novel in the Radclyffe Hall tradition is, it seems, to ignore the diversity of the literary echoes reverberating throughout the text.

Whereas lesbian-feminist critics seem to be in agreement about *Oranges* being an identifiably lesbian novel, their reception of *Written on the Body* has been more mixed. Some suggest it is more radical than *Oranges*—"an outlaw text", Carolyn Allen calls it;[23] others, however, see it in terms of failed opportunities—Patricia Duncker, for example. Still, what seems always to be at issue is the gender-unidentified narrator and the implications he or she has for the text. Is Winterson out to suggest that passion is non-gendered, universal, that "true love" conquers all differences? Or, can the sex of the narrator, as it is suggested by the majority of critics, actually be determined as female ?

Written is a love story, a romance of sorts, and as such it depends upon two gender-identified lovers, Allen argues. Thus, the reader is compelled to "sex" the narrator. While Allen never loses sight of the fact that sexual indeterminacy haunts the text—"the specter of a male lover defends against the anxiety of

---

[21] The distinction between priest and prophet is an important one. Whereas with the priest the meaning of the word is stabilized by reference to God, with the prophet words are allowed free play. This distinction is parallel to the one made in "Deuteronomy"—the theoretical heart of the novel—between history— words abused in the name of power, and story—always indeterminate and unfixed. Winterson, of course, comes down strongly on the side of stories.

[22] Lyn Pykett, "A New Way with Words?: Jeanette Winterson's Post-Modernism", in *'I'm telling you stories': Jeanette Winterson and the Politics of Reading*, eds. Helena Grice and Tim Woods (Amsterdam and Atlanta: Rodopi, 1998), p. 58.

[23] Carolyn Allen, *Following Djuna: Women Lovers and the Erotics of Loss* (Bloomington and Indianapolis: Indiana University Press, 1996), p. 16.

identificatory engulfment" (Allen, p. 80)—she still concludes that it remains a ghostly presence. A number of factors—textual and extra-textual—leads her to determine the sex of the narrator as female. Not only is Winterson a professed lesbian, her best-known novel, *Oranges,* is also an explicitly lesbian novel, and *Written* itself abounds with references to mirrors, twins, and doublings (Allen, p. 48).[24] In a complex, and in many ways brilliant, analysis of the "erotics of risk" at work in both *The Passion* and *Written,* Allen suggests that Winterson "eroticize[s] not only resemblance, but also the risks inherent in likeness between lovers" (Allen, p. 19). In her view, *Written* deals with the problem in lesbian relationships of retaining some kind of otherness between two like lovers: in what way is the other other? Through risk—of loss of lover as well as of self, of intimacy and commitment—an element of otherness is introduced, and thus functions as a defence against mere self-projection. Allen's arguments are very perceptive, but what *Written* says about the risks of passion—the fear of being read like an "open book" by the lover, of losing oneself in the beloved other, or, of simply losing control—seems a more general statement about the ambiguous nature of love: at once wonderfully powerful, because potentially liberating, but also terribly risky. The same could be said about Allen's contention that "[t]he language of difference and sameness, incorporation and engulfment, twinning and mirroring promotes a reading of lesbian affective connection" (Allen, p. 76). The rhetoric of such a mystical union—"lovers united in one body or two bodies in one" (Allen, p. 77)—is not exclusive to lesbian literature. In "Jerusalem", for instance, William Blake—visionary and poet, to whom Jeanette compares herself in *Oranges* (p. 41)—writes about men in brotherhood who "walked / To and fro Eternity as One man, reflecting each in each & clearly seen / And seeing".[25] Either way, by insisting on determining the narrator's sex, Allen ultimately denies *Written* the textual play fundamental to the novel at all levels—the play with sexual identity, with romantic discourse, and literary conventions—the result being a clearly unintended stabilization of the text.

Allen, however, is by no means the only one who identifies the love story as a lesbian one. Lamenting the fact that Winterson's lesbianism is often ignored in the reception of her work,[26] as well as the fact that many lesbian-feminists have reviewed *Written* unfavourably, Cath Stowers aims to demonstrate that there is

---

[24] For some examples of mirror images in *Written on the Body*, see pages 99, 120, 132, and 163.

[25] William Blake, *Jerusalem* (chapter 4, *plate 98*, ll. 38 - 40), in *Blake: Complete Writings with Variant Readings,* ed. George Keynes (London: Oxford University Press, 1996), p. 746.

[26] Cath Stowers must be thinking specifically of newspaper reviews. Certainly, the majority of the academic work I have come across—and I have read a great deal—approaches Winterson as a lesbian-feminist writer. Cath Stowers, " The Erupting Lesbian Body: Reading *Written on the Body* as a Lesbian Text", in *'I'm telling you stories': Jeanette Winterson and the Politics of Reading*, eds. Helena Grice and Tim Woods (Amsterdam and Atlanta: Rodopi, 1998).

"a consistent lesbian aesthetic running through her novels" (Stowers, p. 89). She does so in order to "correct ... any tendency that would elevate the meaning of her work to a transcendental or universal realm" (Stowers, p. 89). In particular, Stowers is intent on refuting the common charge that *Written* fails to create a lesbian discourse of desire in which the distinction between subject and object of desire, between self and other, breaks down. Part of Stowers' argument rests on her contention that Winterson has modelled her narrator on the theories of Monique Wittig. Like Wittig's "lesbian", the narrator of *Written* functions as a "sign", or a subject position, beyond gender dichotomies, neither male nor female (Stowers, p. 91). For Stowers, then, Winterson's success in creating a discourse of lesbian desire is, partly at least, determined by her deployment of lesbian theory. This becomes particularly interesting in connection with an article by Patricia Duncker, who voices precisely the charge which Stowers is trying to counter, and does so partly on the grounds that *Written* fails to make full use of Monique Wittig.

"I wrote LESBIANS IGNITE over numerous lavatory walls",[27] Patricia Duncker—a disillusioned radical feminist for whom "lesbian" used to equal women's revolutionary impulse to liberty—writes, and, unwittingly, I am sure, brings to mind the rather amusing portrait of the "anarcha-feminist", Inge, in *Written*. Duncker's article presents a problematic piece of criticism. She seems to write from a conviction that since early feminism created both the context and the readership for Winterson's novels, not to mention the fact that she clearly could not have written her novels without the insights of feminist theory, she somehow owes the lesbian-feminist readership to live up to their critical criteria. She is pleased to find some of the "jubilant crew of man-haters and lesbians" (Duncker, p. 80) of early feminist poetry in some of Winterson's works, but *Written* is a disappointment. Monique Wittig's *The Lesbian Body*—the body as "not only mirrored [but] already shared" (Duncker, p. 84)—she argues, has obvious significant bearing on the middle section of *Written*. In Duncker's view, it is a problem, however, that the lesbian relationship is left undeclared. Her argument is that Winterson's wish (which is a genuine one) to leave open the possibility that the narrator is male, forces her to engage with heterosexual clichés. Regrettably, this means that Louise remains an object of desire. Duncker concludes that

> for this reader at least, *Written on the Body* is a text full of lost opportunities. Winterson refuses to write an 'out' lesbian novel....
> Fair enough. But I think that she is losing more than she gains,

---

[27] Patricia Duncker, "Jeanette Winterson and the Aftermath of Feminism", in *'I'm telling you stories': Jeanette Winterson and the Politics of Reading*, eds. Helena Grice and Tim Woods (Amsterdam and Atlanta: Rodopi, 1998), p. 79.

because the wonderful echo of *The Lesbian Body* stands at the centre of the book ... a monument to what the text might have been (Duncker, p. 85).

While I do, in fact, believe that the lovers in *Written* are successful in transcending the dichotomy between subject and object of desire without them giving up their uniqueness as individuals—both are at various times described in terms of map-makers or inscribers of desire as well as map-readers or translators of desire[28]—what concerns me is the way that Duncker seems to "impose" theory on *Written*. At the same time that Duncker acknowledges Winterson's intention to leave the narrator's sex indeterminate, she faults her for failing to "sex" the narrator because this directly results in a failure to revision Wittig's work. Stowers and Duncker appear in the same collection of critical essays on Winterson. In their introduction to the collection, the editors argue that the "essays allow readers to see how theory and text can interact".[29] It is their theoretical stance that "[t]he fiction is always performing and enacting a theoretical position; whilst theory is always offering a practical position from which to act" (Grice and Woods, p. 3). Duncker's essay suggests that this latter point does not always hold true.

"Listen for the Author's Voice", the first half of my title suggests. While it has not been the intention of this article to present a critique of lesbian-feminist criticism in general, implicit in this suggestion is nevertheless a more general critique of the way much "contemporary" literary criticism—including feminism— approaches literary texts. The past thirty years have seen a proliferation of literary theories which have brought some profound changes to literary studies. The notion of literature has been dissolved into a concept of various "discursive practices", the Author has been replaced by the reader/s, and literary criticism seems no longer subordinate to the literary texts studied. Hans Hauge in "The Ethical Demand" regrets especially two things about the critical climate today: that attention is directed away from primary texts and that ethics has replaced aesthetics in novel reading.[30] Winterson would agree, I am sure, but, more importantly, her texts seem to demand that the reader/critic listens hard for an Authorial voice. Even if we cannot speak of the Author's intention—and I think the death of the Author was a welcome one (even if Winterson greatly complicates

---

[28] See, for example, pages 29, 52, 89, and 106.

[29] Helena Grice and Tim Woods, "Reading Winterson's Writing", in *'I'm telling you stories': Jeanette Winterson and the Politics of Reading*, eds. Helena Grice and Tim Woods (Amsterdam and Atlanta: Rodopi, 1998), p. 3.

[30] Hans Hauge, "The Ethical Demand: Responding to J. Hillis Miller's 'The Roar on the Other Side of Silence: Otherness in *Middlemarch*'", *Edda*, (1995), p. 247.

this matter)—surely, there is the intention of the text to reckon with. Not only is Winterson's fiction full of theory,[31] it is also full of echoes of literary ancestors. Winterson hates the Canon, but she loves the tradition from which she always writes, and which she would like her reader/critic to pay attention to more than to any abstract theories. Contrary to many feminists, Winterson does not seem to suffer from any anxieties, whether of influence or authorship.[32] "I do not feel trapped in any way by language. I don't feel that it's a male language that I have to deal with", she says in an interview.[33] In Bloomian terms Winterson is a brilliant "mispriser"; influenced but by no means anxious.

Hence, while I think that literary studies have been greatly improved by much contemporary theory, and also acknowledge that there is no such thing as "theory-free" criticism, it does seem from some of the examples discussed that assumptions about what a lesbian writer ought to write intrude between the text and the critic; in effect, that the work is being judged by the writer (in particular her sexuality) as well as by theory, rather than the writer being judged by the work. When so many critics "sex" the ungendered narrator of *Written on the Body*, they specifically go against the intention of the text to create a space in which the whole point is that gender may be variously constructed, but is ultimately left indeterminate. "What matters is that there's a space created in the text into which a male and female consciousness can enter and be redefined", Winterson states in an interview (Bush, p. 55). "I don't think that viewing sex from an androgynous model is necessarily a good idea but I do think there's too much emphasis put on gender" (Winterson quoted by Bush, p. 55).[34] In fact, lesbian-feminism's emphasis on gender often seems concomitant with an

---

[31] For example the "Deuteronomy" chapter in *Oranges*—a kind of artistic credo. Patricia Waugh notes in *Harvest of the Sixties* (Oxford: Oxford University Press, 1995) that the realistic novel began to lose ground in the 1970s, and from there took a fantastic turn, writers "often combining a magic use of spatial and temporal dislocation with essayistic narratorial intrusion" (p. 179). She mentions writers such as A.S. Byatt, David Lodge, John Fowles, Julian Barnes, Angela Carter, and Jeanette Winterson as examples of this new mode of writing

[32] Here I am, of course, alluding to Harold Bloom's theory of "creative revisionism" and Gilbert and Gubar's appropriation of it for a feminist criticism. Bloom mentions both in his introduction to *Lesbian and Bisexual Women Writers* (1997: p. xi).

[33] Catherine Bush, "Why is the measure of love loss?: Interview with Jeanette Winterson", *Bomb*, spring, 1993, p. 57.

[34] At the same time that the narrator of *Written* is not androgynous, Winterson does seem to celebrate some kind of double-gendered being as an ideal. Patricia Waugh suggests we may read Fortunata in *Sexing* as "an image of romantic yearning for discovery of and completion by the other which will return us to a primordial and pristine self undivided by gender". Patricia Waugh, *Harvest of the Sixties*. (Oxford: Oxford University Press, 1995), p. 194. In *Art & Lies* androgyny is, of course, very much manifested in the figure of Handel—a castrato. "Woman had been taken out of man. Why not put her back into man? ... The perfect man. *Male and female He created him*" (pp. 195 - 196, my emphasis).

emphasis on "sameness", that is, an assumption that all lesbian-feminists are essentially the same; that they write alike, read alike, and share the same experiences and goals. In this way the lesbian-feminist ideology becomes in a sense itself an oppressive one. Certainly, for Winterson "the question is not so much what it is like to be a woman [or a lesbian], but what it is like to be an individual" (Hansson, p. 36). Hence, "feminism as a political alternative in a totalising manner" is never endorsed (Hansson, p. 36).

As this article has taken the form of a critique, I have only indirectly managed to suggest what I think one may unravel from Winterson's writing by approaching it in a different way. Instead of reading her in a particular conceptual framework, I propose that by delving into her body of work—by listening hard for the Author's voice—a "Wintersonian poetics" may be discovered. In his introduction to Jeanette Winterson in *Lesbian and Bisexual Women Writers* Harold Bloom says that "[a]s a writer of lesbian fiction, she is commonly viewed as representative of a new phase, in which the traditional emphasis on self-discovery and self-affirmation has shifted to a broader examination of the nature of humanity itself" (Bloom, p. 137). I agree with everything but the "commonly viewed", which has yet to materialize. As I have tried to suggest by way of contrast, Jeanette Winterson is a writer very much taken up with philosophical questions where sex is endlessly significant, but not confined to the directly political. Central to her writing seems to be ontological questions about the creation of identity and the nature of humanity, and, in relation to these, two very significant concerns are those of love and language.[35] For Winterson, transcendence—going beyond oneself in search for an "other"— is absolutely essential for the creation of a person, and both art and love seem to carry with them a promise of transformation, of transcendence. Winterson's concept of transpersonality in art, the artist seeking expression—language—which is "[o]f me, but not me" (*A&L*, p. 139), and which therefore possesses a unifying energy, is also applicable to her idea of love. Love, too, transforms and unites—the lover is at once self and other, and thus created as a whole person through love. Like art, "[o]f me but not me" (*A&L*, p. 139).

The "Wintersonian poetics", then, seems to be that books are the space in which desire can be explored. Desire creates "cities of the interior" which "do not lie on any map" (*The Passion*, pp. 114, 150, 152). It is a highly sexy, but not specifically gendered space and irreducible to mapping by way of gender politics or philosophical dualism. It is the space of stories. "[T]here's only art and lies" (*A&L*, p. 69), and Winterson's are of the very best.

---

[35] The parallel is explicitly pinpointed in *Art Objects,* p. 15. See also Marianne Børch, "Love's Ontology and the Problem of Cliché" in this volume.

The Vast, Unmappable Cities of the Interior:
Place and Passion in *The Passion*

by Helene Bengtson

In Winterson's short story "Orion" (from *The World and Other Places*), the protagonist Artemis "found that the whole world could be contained in one place because that place was herself" (p. 57). A similar observation could be made about the Venice of *The Passion*, which becomes an elaborate expression of the passion(s) of those who live there.

Another pertinent passage, found in *Gut Symmetries*, has strong echoes of the bewildering Venetian experience and describes in itself Winterson's many-faceted use of place at a very basic level: "[w]hat should be stable, shifts. What I am told is solid, slips. The sensible strong ordinary world of fixity is a folklore" (*GutS*, p. 10).

In *The Passion,* the fantastic city of Venice is presented to the reader as an ever-changing labyrinth which can never be navigated the same way twice. It contains the "cities of the interior"—a phrase which not only covers the hidden waterways that only boatmen know, but also, symbolically, the realm of human passion (pp. 68, 114, 150, 152). The aim of this essay is to explore "the cities of the interior" of the two narrators in *The Passion* and describe the way in which the characters' interior workings inform their perception of their surroundings—particularly Venice, which is depicted as a living, strongly symbolic organism resisting any attempt at mapping and rationalisation. That use of "symbolic

Thanks to Marianne Børch and Cindie Aaen Maagaard for their helpful suggestions, the importance of which cannot be exaggerated.

17

spread",[1] partly drawn from the great quest narratives of a literary past that Winterson so obviously hails, is present in all of her work, from *The World and Other Places* and all the way back to the romance tales inserted in *Oranges Are Not the Only Fruit*: "[Winnet] thinks she doesn't change anything as she looks, but she must, because every time she goes round, the same things are different" (*Oranges,* p. 155).

The custom-made geography of romance quests, with an adventure and a lady for each knight, has much in common with the fluid Venetian topography that meets Henri and Villanelle in *The Passion*: the Venetian cityscape is a testing-ground which, like the dangerous wilderness of chivalric romance, supplies the challenges which will bring out the errant knight's merit. Where, however, the traditional romances have very strict, binary divisions of space (hostile/friendly~wilderness/court), Winterson's dialogic, postmodern romance is out to do away with such simplified patterns and suggests instead a multiple reality based on personal perception and emotion, and relatively unbound by linear conventions of space and time. Those concepts, and many others, are laid out in several personalised versions, with no implication that any one of them is to be accepted automatically as correct, neutral or objective. (Yet, Winterson can by no means be accused of relativism; her values are always deducible, but she does not believe in ready-made solutions, as she already stated in *Oranges*, comparing the priest, who "has a book with the words set out", to the prophet, who "has no book" [p. 156]). What Winterson emphasises is the singularity of personal perception which affects one's experience of place. For instance, what is enemy territory to the protagonists as they walk from Moscow to Venice is home to the people they meet and deceive into helping them. As Henri remarks: "it seems we are as we appear. What nonsense we make of our hatreds when we can only recognise them in the most obvious circumstances" (p. 105). The authority of objectively measured physical distance is also challenged: "[o]ur village was not very far down the Seine, but we might as well have been living on the moon" (p. 16).[2] When it comes to Venice, of course, Henri and Villanelle have very different perceptions of the same city, as the following exchange shows: -"This is a living city. Things change." -"Villanelle, cities don't." -"Henri, they do" (p. 113). Eventually, Henri adopts an attitude similar to that of Villanelle; not, however,

---

[1] Northrop Frye defines the symbolic spread as "the sense that a work of literature is expanding into insights and experiences beyond itself". Northrop Frye, *The Secular Scripture: A Study of the Structure of Romance* (Cambridge, Massachusetts and London: Harvard University Press, 1976), p. 59.

[2] One example of double vision concerns a whole story, namely that of Villanelle, which is first narrated by herself in her own chapter ("The Queen of Spades") and then presented to the reader as Henri's memory of what she told him and Patrick in "The Zero Winter". (That title is itself a juxtaposition: it originates in Eliot's "Little Gidding": "the unimaginable zero *summer*" [my emphasis], ll. 19 - 20.)

because he has been forced or persuaded by her, but because he has experienced the truth of it himself.

In Venice, Winterson has found one of the Western world's most beguiling cities to serve as the "interactive" backdrop for her fiction. The mythical element of water, leading traditionally to insight and metamorphosis, is a vital presence,[3] not least because it provides the "other"-world of the waterways with their obvious allusions to the unconscious and repressed parts of the human psyche. Winterson exploits the city's inherent semantics of romance and paradox to the full, utilising the air of magic to sustain a fantastic Venetian mythology in which the dead clichés of our common (in both senses of the word) language are restored to life: the streets of the city literally change places overnight; love literally makes Villanelle walk on water, and her loving heart is literally in someone else's possession, existing and beating independently of her body until Henri can steal it back for her to swallow. The effect is, in Winterson's own words, that of "an imaginative reality sufficiently at odds with our daily reality to startle us out of it" (*Art Objects*, p. 188).

In the above quotation it is important to note that we are dealing with two kinds of reality: an "imaginative" and a "daily" one (or the "real lives" [note the plural] offered by art versus the "actual life" of "daily insignificance" [*ArtOb*, p. 59]). "Realism" is incompatible with art in Winterson's view, and she describes the true artist as someone "in full possession of a reality less partial than the reality of most people" (*ArtOb*, p. 168). The "strange distorting looking-glass" (*ArtOb*, p. 150) of her art, in line with the modernist thinking of her most influential predecessors, presents truth as subjective, unstable ("no emotion is the final one", *Oranges* p. 48) and created by means of both imagination and emotion. Thus the story of Joséphine's prison garden is true because it comforts Henri, and his and Villanelle's "trust me" stories are true because they are a more effective way of getting at their identities than any regurgitation of facts, no matter how "accurate".[4]

A truth that lasts, in the form of stories, or art (*ArtOb* epigraph), is a recognisable ideal throughout Winterson's work, and the multiple truths offered by stories inevitably affect the notion of place in the oeuvre: "[t]he earth is not flat and neither is reality" (*ArtOb*, p. 151). Venice as symbol is not a one-tenor-one-vehicle relationship; it is a many-headed mercurial paradigm of

---

[3] This is also the case in other of Winterson's novels: the Thames is a crucial link between the two Londons of *Sexing the Cherry*, and the New York of *Gut Symmetries* relies on the Hudson river as well as the Atlantic Ocean for its alchemic qualities. Finally it is worth remembering that each of the three cities is built on an island, a chronotopic entity with many parallels to that of the boat, or, by extension, the conceit of the Ship of Fools.

[4] For a discussion of storytelling and identity in *Sexing the Cherry*, see Bente Gade's essay "Multiple Selves and Grafted Agents" in this collection.

meaning revolving around the nature(s) of passion. The key to its interpretation is subjectivity or point of view: as a reflecting medium, almost a "mirror perilous", Venice reveals what it is held up against.[5]

The feminine aspects of the city have been dealt with by several critics to such an extent that I find no grounds for elaboration.[6] But I should like to direct attention to Venice as a signifier of passion which crosses sex and gender divisions. "The city of" a large number of things, such as "mazes" (p. 49), "disguises" (p. 56) and "uncertainty" (p. 58), offers, by force of its paradoxical nature,[7] an expression of the almost inexpressible: the passion that is strong enough to rock the foundations of what one believed to be oneself. <u>The passionate desire for the other</u> is ultimately a search for the completed self, as suggested in the following passage:

> I had begun to feel that this city contained only two people who sensed each other and never met. Whenever I went out I hoped and dreaded to see the other. In the faces of strangers I saw one face and in the mirror I saw my own (p. 97).[8]

The gambling motif, another way of expressing passion in *The Passion*, similarly involves mirroring: "[t]he two men met each other's gaze for a moment before they seated themselves in front of the dominoes and in each face was something of the other" (p. 93). The mirroring taking place here is tangible, even bodily, as opposed to the merely optical reflection in a glass surface. The perceived reality of Venice, like a chivalric romance landscape, meets, or mirrors, the merits and desires of the "quester" in the same three-dimensional way.

---

[5] As with the living statue of Queen Hermione in Shakespeare's *The Winter's Tale*, "[i]t is required you do awake your faith". This can be read as a metatextual statement of the necessity to fully engage in the novel's fictional universe, as well as a recognition of the fact that passion is not possible if doubted. William Shakespeare, *The Winter's Tale*, ed. Ernest Schanzer (London: Penguin, 1969, 1996), p. 158 (V, 3, 94 - 5) and *The Passion*, p. 49.

[6] For instance, Paulina Palmer describes Winterson's Venice as "a symbolic representation of a feminine erotic economy" and explains that "[t]he shifting perspectives which [Winterson] ascribes to the city, along with the connections it displays with water, relate it to femininity and the fluctuating nature of desire". Paulina Palmer, "*The Passion*: Storytelling, Fantasy, Desire", in '*I'm telling you stories': Jeanette Winterson and the Politics of Reading,* eds. Helena Grice and Tim Woods (Amsterdam and Atlanta: Rodopi, 1998), p. 113.

[7] One of the paradoxical elements of the city is the Rialto bridge, which can be drawn up to form a barrier instead of passage. If it were to be sealed, it would be "the doom of paradox" (p. 61).

[8] The idea of the other being a "missing part" of the subject's self is also present in *Sexing the Cherry*, where Jordan, in the process of looking for Fortunata, finds himself (see e.g. pp. 40, 80, 102 - 3). Henri also describes falling in love as seeing himself for the first time (*The Passion*, p. 154).

Judith Seaboyer in her excellent essay on *The Passion* describes Venice as "a figure for two privileged and inextricably linked psychoanalytic tropes: death and the body of a woman" and maintains that Henri, one of the two protagonist narrators, "remains an exile unable to navigate the labyrinth [of Venice] and is swallowed up into madness and despair".[9] While I cannot disprove her very well-based interpretations, I do feel that a more positive aspect should be included, not least because Seaboyer unquestioningly accepts Villanelle's version of Henri's behaviour.[10] That approach is arguably risky when dealing with a dialogic novel: there does not appear to be any one authoritative narrator as the two take turns at interrupting one another, and for formal as well as content-related reasons, Henri cannot be overlooked.[11] He is the frame narrator, and we know his exact position in place and narration-time; the Rock of San Servelo, "now" (i.e., 1821 or later), from which he invokes his past in analeptic passages partly sustained by his little journal. Villanelle's location is harder to establish, and she might even have been put in by Henri—on at least one occasion, in the fire-and-tale scene (p. 89), she definitely has. Villanelle's vision of Venice as perpetually changing remains essentially unaltered, while Henri's attitude to the city shifts from one of bewildered powerlessness to one of feeling at home—a development which obviously stems from a thoroughgoing change in his perception of himself. Finally, he introduces the main refrains ("I'm telling you stories. Trust me", p. 5; "You play, you win, you play, you lose. You play" and "what you risk reveals what you value", p. 43); Villanelle repeats them (a villanelle being a very repetitive type of poem)[12] and adds a fourth: "the valuable fabulous thing" (p. 90).

Mythmaker that she is, Villanelle's rendition of events is always very appealing, but in Winterson's universe, the authority of myth should not be taken without a grain of salt, and Villanelle does indirectly confess to imposing her own standards on her view of Henri's actions, "opening his door with [her] own key as [she] always did" (p. 149).[13] Importantly, Henri remains in Venice "by choice" (p. 152), and his interpretation of freedom profoundly undermines the significance of physical "fact", as does Venice: "To love someone else enough to forget about yourself even for one moment is to be free" (p. 154). Henri also

---

[9] See Judith Seaboyer, "Second Death in Venice: Romanticism and the Compulsion to Repeat in Jeanette Winterson's *The Passion*", *Contemporary Literature* XXXVIII, 3 (1997), pp. 483 - 510 (p. 485).

[10] Louise Humphries, who has written "Listening for the Author's Voice: Un-Sexing the Wintersonian Oeuvre" in this volume, informs me that this is a general tendency in Winterson criticism.

[11] Dialogism has an effective advocate in Henri, as he says: "There are voices and they must be heard" (p. 142).

[12] —as Judith Seaboyer, among others, also notes (Seaboyer, pp. 493 - 94).

[13] Villanelle also misinterprets Henri at an earlier point in the narrative, mistaking his wish to know more about her home-town Venice for a desire to find an appropriate disguise (pp. 99 - 100).

recognises the desire of the physical body as a source of freedom, balancing body and mind:[14]

> The mystics and the churchmen talk about throwing off this body and its desires, being no longer a slave to the flesh. They don't say that through the flesh we are set free. That our desire for another will lift us out of ourselves more cleanly than anything divine (p. 154).

Henri craves freedom—including the freedom to make his own mistakes (pp. 86, 157)—but this is not possible for him until he has discovered that he himself is the all-powerful one in relation to his own destiny. A funny detail here is the tiny Alice-in-Wonderland-like bottle of "[essence] of great value and potency" (p. 120) which Henri pockets from the closet belonging to the "Queen of Spades", a character associated with destiny,[15] while retrieving Villanelle's lost heart. After this event, which can be interpreted as a classic romance test (in this version requiring Henri to let go of his narrow, matter-of-fact view of language and reality), he becomes able to *act* in the Venetian cityscape and control his own fate, as if the essence in his pocket has helped him, although we never hear of it again.

As mentioned above, it is crucial for the understanding of Venice's function in *The Passion* to take into consideration which of the two equally important narrators we are listening to at any given moment: Villanelle is the one who creates the fabulous legend of Venice, backed by her parents,[16] whereas Henri's version of the same city is far more prosaic and reserved, at least to begin with. He even has the nerve to suggest that Villanelle is being "deliberately mysterious" about the Venetian topography, showing him a route that he, as a stranger to the place, would never be able to recognise. With her answer she proves him right without admitting it, saying that she is "taking [him] down an ancient way that only a boatman could hope to remember" (p. 113). She creates *her* Venice in her own, ambiguous image, playfully manipulating oppositions such as land/water, male/female, hidden/visible, inner/outer to display a city, and a self, that is "never

---

[14] This experience echoes that of Jeanette in *Oranges*. In order to remain a whole person, she has to turn her back on her religious society, which defines the divine and true as something purely spiritual, classifying the "flesh" and all that goes with it as "unholy". A dream reveals to her that "[t]he body that contains a spirit is the one true god" (*Oranges*, p. 110).

[15] Villanelle, when talking about her feelings for the "Queen of Spades", likens her passion to destiny (p. 62). The mysterious lady plans and stages their affair, makes destiny-tapestries (p. 121), has her coffin set out (p. 119) and is married to a map-man. She is a controlling and omniscient ("books two deep", p. 119) power in her relationship with Villanelle and, in my opinion, qualifies as a fully allegorical romance character.

[16] This allusion to "poetic ancestry" has a counterpart on pages 61 - 2, where a passage strongly reminiscent of T.S. Eliot muses on the role of ancestry in Venice and the nature of time.

still" (pp. 110, 123), somewhere humanly "between God and the Devil", somewhere passionately "between fear and sex" (p. 68).

That Villanelle is seen almost exclusively in public spaces is one instance of how several conventional gender rules are transgressed.[17] Her Venetian chronotopes are the traditionally masculine ones of motion (boats), money and risk (the casino), and public appearance (streets and squares). In line with Villanelle's androgynous identity, these masculine chronotopes, alluding typically to the carnivalesque literature from before the eighteenth-century rise of the novel, are described by means of the intimate first-person narration which suited the novelistic female narrators and their domesticated use of space so well.[18] Villanelle's association with the carnivalesque view of the world counterbalances Henri's association with the more official versions of it: he believes in road signs, maps, and truthful recordings of past feelings; and he attempts, at first, to rationalise Venice's fantastic qualities as good stories and bad city planning. He prefers the domestic chronotopes and combines the intimate personal narration with something which, at first glance, resembles history-writing—a traditionally male mode. However, like Jordan in *Sexing*, Henri deals in the marginal (hi)stories that would not otherwise be told and thus also belongs within the boundaries of the carnivalesque.

The carnivalesque feature is emphasised by means of another chronotope pertaining to Henri: that of the lunatic asylum, which he also domesticates and feminises, evoking the smell of porridge and his mother quietly cooking it (p. 135). An article by Suzanne Rosenthal Shumway explores the subversive effects of the madhouse chronotope on the primary narrative in *Jane Eyre*, and it is interesting to see that Winterson has given the narrative hierarchies thus implied a disturbing twist, using Henri´s discourse from the asylum as a frame for the perceived sanity (however fantastic) of Villanelle's narrative. The madhouse is a chosen residence for Henri, and whereas the madness in *Jane Eyre* works towards dissolving language and narrative, Henri's being madly in love is the inspiration

---

[17] Villanelle is the epitome of gender as construct, combining a beautiful female body with "masculine" webbed feet and a boatman's skill and strength. She cross-dresses, at work as well as in private, and has what must be seen as a conventionally masculine talent for using maps and compass. She has, unsuccessfully, been a wife and, successfully, becomes a mother. For a brief discussion of the mixed gender features of Henri and Villanelle, see for instance M. Daphne Kutzer, "The Cartography of Passion: Cixous, Wittig and Winterson", in *Re-Naming the Landscape*, eds. Jürgen Kleist and Bruce Butterfield (New York: Peter Lang, 1994), pp. 133 - 45, esp. 137 - 9. An entire article devoted to the subject is María del Mar Asensio's "Subversion of Sexual Identity in Jeanette Winterson's *The Passion*", in *Gender, I-deology: Essays on Theory, Fiction and Film*, eds. Chantal Cornut Gentille D'Arcy and José Angel García Landa (Amsterdam and Atlanta: Rodopi, 1996), pp. 265 - 79.

[18] I have made use of Sue Vice's *Introducing Bakhtin* (Manchester: Manchester University Press, 1997), ch. 5.

for his narrative, annihilating the constraints of space and time and creating language of a very poetic and powerful kind. Thus, in containing the rest of the textual universe, and because madness will usually be conceived as representing the opposite of sanity or normality, "the chronotope of the asylum works to invert the reader's concepts of gender, of space, even of time"[19] as it sets other standards and enforces their validity through application.

To all intents and purposes, Villanelle and Henri narrate very differently: Villanelle *is* poetry (hence her name) and in a sense Henri's muse; Henri the writer who grapples with the natures of passion and obsession as illustrated in his progress from an immature worship of Napoleon to an adult, selfless love for Villanelle. The burning of Moscow illustrates Henri's painfully changed attitude towards his leader: "Moscow is a city of domes, … a city of squares and worship.… It was a difficult city to burn" (pp. 83 - 84). When out on his own in Venice, Henri sees churches everywhere, and even the "rational" public garden—Napoleon's creation—can, on a foggy night, muster "four sepulchral churches" (p. 112) as a reminiscence of his previous worship.[20]

The progression in Henri's approach to Venice is very clearly demonstrated in his choice of words. Still not quite over Napoleon and his view of the world as an object to be controlled, Henri "[gets] lost from the first" (p. 112) when he arrives in Venice, which he describes as a "city of madmen" (pp. 112, 121) and "an impossible maze" (p. 110). He does not believe his senses, communicating his dominant impressions by using the word "seem" (pp. 109 - 10) and likening Venice to "an invented city" (p. 109). The churches that tauntingly pop up around him are a response to his search for a home, more specifically the home of Villanelle's family, where he has been warmly welcomed, but as her brother (pp. 113, 136). He is at that point, as the churches also reveal, still a worshipper, and therefore the control of his life hinges on the beloved other, Villanelle. When Henri finally finds her, he asks her for a map, which she claims is an impossibility when dealing with Venice.[21] Instead, she gives him a tour of the town, or rather a lesson in life: "Leave plenty of time in your doings and be prepared to go another way, to do something not planned if that is where the streets lead you" (p. 113).

---

[19] Suzanne Rosenthal Shumway, "The Chronotope of the Asylum: *Jane Eyre*, Feminism, and Bakhtinian Theory" in *A Dialogue of Voices*: *Feminist Literary Theory and Bakhtin*, eds. Karen Hohne and Helen Wussov (Minneapolis and London: University of Minnesota Press, 1994), pp. 152 - 170. I quote from p. 158.

[20] They also constitute a link to Henri's new passion, Villanelle, who loved those same four churches (p. 52).

[21] As Thomas L. Dumm notes, writing about the implications of the recently invented, exact satellite-aided positioning: "The primary paradox unveiled by the GPS [the Navstar Global Positioning System] is this: To be precisely located on a map is a new way of being lost. Once it is plotted with precision on a grid, location at a site is displaced by representation in cyberspace. This abstraction

Villanelle the poem educates Henri the man, telling him that "[t]he cities of the interior do not lie on any map" (p. 114) and returning to him not only Domino's talisman, which he believed to have been lost, but miraculously also the icicle which had naturally enough formed itself around the gold in the Russian winter— a signifier of believing the impossible. As mentioned, that is exactly what Henri is required to do in order to find his beloved's missing heart. When he does, Villanelle rewards him with a miraculous heart-swallowing—another attack on disbelief, but not the returned favour Henri had hoped for: "[T]here was something I wanted too; why had she never taken her boots off?" (p. 109).

It is necessary for Henri to kill Villanelle's husband, the former army cook, before he can have his true miracle—one that not only reveals to him the most intimate core of Villanelle's identity, but also ends his exile and estrangement: "I … saw Villanelle, … walking on the canal and dragging our boats. Her boots lay neatly one by the other. Her hair was down. I was in the red forest and she was leading me home" (p. 129).[22] "The red forest" is used as a metaphor for the body (cf. the heart as a "blue stone in a red forest" [p. 138]), so, again, Henri seems to be moving towards a more unified identity; one that adds to his previous moral existence a physical side which gives him more personal authority. As Villanelle remarks about this past self of his: "He had no notion of what men do, he had no notion of what his own body did until I showed him" (p. 148).

Henri's understanding of gambling—and thus also of passion and life— leaps forward from the childish noughts and crosses (pp. 43, 136) to the grown-up "card game" of the pivotal point of his existence: "And for the first time in my life I realised that I was the powerful one. I was the one who held the wild card" (p. 138). From this epiphany on, Henri is a whole person *to himself*, and his imprisonment in San Servelo gives him a home where he chooses to stay although he is given the chance to leave, recognising that freedom is not a matter of physical space. He explains: "I don't ever want to be alone again and I don't want to see any more of the world. *The cities of the interior are vast and do not lie on any map*" (p. 152, my emphasis).

"Orion", the short story cited at the beginning of this essay, has more wisdom to offer on the subject of what a change in self-perception does to a person's perception of the world: "And so it is with the mind that it moves from

---

of space has profound consequences at the level of experience". He adds to this that being lost opens the mind to new possibilities. Thomas L. Dumm, *Michel Foucault and the Politics of Freedom* (Thousand Oaks, London and New Delhi: Sage Publications, 1996), p. 30. Being "lost in a strange town" is, in the novel's value system, an epitome of human existence (*The Passion,* p. 139) and therefore a necessary experience on the way towards that "freedom to make [one's] own mistakes" which Henri is looking for (pp. 86, 157).

[22] Another "red forest" on page 121 emphasises Henri's exile and his and Villanelle's miscommunication, as it is still "*her* red forest" (my emphasis).

its prison to a free and vast plain without any movement at all. Something new has entered the process" (*World*, p. 58).

As mentioned, many critics, perhaps influenced by the perceived feminism of Winterson's oeuvre, have read a judgement of the two protagonists into the way she portrays them and see Villanelle as positive, perceptive and powerful, Henri as a powerless fiasco who fails to understand life, women and passion. But there are numerous parallels between their actions. Thus when Henri chooses not to see Villanelle, it is as valid as her choosing not to see the "Queen of Spades". They both acknowledge the existence of ghosts (Villanelle pp. 61 - 2, 76)—an obvious reference to artistic ancestry—and Henri's home on San Servelo is as true and good to him as Villanelle's home in the city, or cities, of Venice. This is the message from the Romantic era—influenced by the ideals of the early part of the French Revolution—in which the novel is set: Henri and Villanelle are equal (and equally free), and their personal experiences are all-important.

In Henri's last remark about Venice, he still maintains that it is a city "of madmen", an epithet which has now been semantically re-coded by the fact that he acknowledges the madness that love is and lives in what is literally a madhouse. His contemplative imprisonment and "Trojan Horse" of a poetic journal have shown him "the difference between inventing a lover and falling in love" (p. 158),[23] and he chooses to remain suspended in his textual universe, forever in love with his muse, now having realised that Venice, and by implication also the realm of human passion, is "a living city" (p. 158) in which anything can happen.

Thus the lover's true home is not a physical place, but his or her love, requited or unrequited, and Henri's book of stories about his passion is, also, arguably a celebration of the common genealogy of artists and lovers:[24] his recognition of the value and inherent freedom in being able to love has strong affinities with Winterson's writings about art, as love and art both exist independently of acceptance: "whether it is loved or it is not, it is the same piece of work. Reaction cannot alter what is written. And what is written is the writer's true home" (*ArtOb*, p. 179).

[23] Winterson, when talking about her use of fantastic plot(s) in *The Passion*, suggests: "Might we be back at the Trojan Horse?" (*ArtOb*, p. 189). She first used the image to describe the device of fiction masked as autobiography (that of Gertrude Stein's *Autobiography of Alice B. Toklas*) and also mentions Wordsworth as the best example of "a writer re-ordering his own identity for the purposes of a poem" (*ArtOb*, p. 57). Arguably, this is what Henri does: "understand[ing] [himself] as fully as [he] can" (*ArtOb*, p. 60) through fiction. This Wordsworthian "real solid world of images" (cited in *ArtOb*, p. 60) is echoed twice in the novel, thus blurring and questioning the boundaries between fiction and fact (*The Passion*, pp. 27, 146).

[24] Susana Onega has a brilliant account of the Borgesian traits in *The Passion*, including Henri's journal as a textual labyrinth which "becomes the path for the hero's quest, and so, his world". Susana Onega, "*The Passion*: Jeanette Winterson's Uncanny Mirror of Ink", *Miscelánea* (Zaragoza), 14 (1993), pp. 113 - 29.

Multiple Selves and Grafted Agents:
A Postmodernist Reading of *Sexing the Cherry*
by Bente Gade

Jeanette Winterson's novel, *Sexing the Cherry*, is a fabulous narrative that challenges general perceptions of reality and destabilises our notion of time and matter. This seductive text makes us wonder what is "real" and how the real is best represented. *Sexing* is teeming with stories of the gigantic Dog Woman, perverse puritans, flying princesses, houses with only ceilings and no floors, places where words are more material than the body, and so on. These wondrous stories are told by different narrators and in challenging the conventional stabilisers, time and matter, they also destabilise identity. At the beginning of the novel the narrator Jordan makes it his ambition to record the journeys *not* undertaken instead of telling the story of the journeys he *had* made. The reason why he makes this apparently bizarre declaration is that "[e]very journey conceals another journey within its lines: the path not taken and the forgotten angle" (p. 9). The point is that this "other journey", which he "might have made, or perhaps did make in some other place or time", is just as important as *real* journeys that may be represented in diaries and on maps. Likewise, identity is restricted by conventional forms of representation that exclude important aspects of individual experiences. According to Jordan, his life is "written invisibly" and "squashed between the facts". In order to know himself better, he decides "to set a watch on [him-]self like a jealous father, trying to catch [him-]self disappearing through a door just noticed in the wall" (p. 10). Jordan's ambition to record his secret inner life opens the novel and unleashes the question of identity and adequate ways of representing it. Thus

Sexing releases a queer exploration of identity that resonates with postmodernist perceptions of the human subject.

My impression of a correspondence between postmodernist theory and Jeanette Winterson's writing shall inform the following reading of *Sexing*. By reading Winterson's text as embodying postmodernist theories I hope to clarify some implications of a postmodernist position. Postmodernism is not a unified school or theory but may be described as critical strategies that are unified by critique of grand, universal theories.[1] Postmodernist critics share the perception that everything is a representation, or in the often cited words of the French philosopher Jacques Derrida: *il n'y a pas de hors-texte*—"[t]here is nothing outside of the text".[2] Textuality eliminates the idea of self-identical entities that may be represented, as everything is characterised by *différance* (Derrida's hybrid of "difference" and "deferral"). Likewise the French historian of ideas Michel Foucault claims that we only need to transcend our *faith* in metaphysics and we will no longer find pure essence behind things, but "the secret that they have no essence or that their essence was fabricated"[3]—hence the imperative to focus analysis upon discourse rather than the essential truths they claim to represent.

A related postmodernist perception is the omnipresence of power. Power is a heterogeneous and intangible network; it is not a substance that can be held or seized, but a relation that is immanent to all other relations. Power is implicated in every representation, because any identity, in order to appear coherent, needs to obscure the exclusion of difference whereupon it depends. Thus representation is never direct but always marked by the constructive role of language. Power is also intimately involved in the process of becoming a subject, as the subject is discursively constituted.[4] The body is the direct locus of domination and it only becomes intelligible through discourse. However, discourse does not merely make our bodies accessible but determines what we *know* of our inner selves. The gap that Winterson's character Jordan senses between representation (the "facts" of

---

[1] Instead of universal theories, which obliterate local workings of power, Michel Foucault advocates a critical technique which he terms "genealogy". The genealogist rediscovers "subjugated knowledges" of struggle and conflict (*Power/Knowledge: Selected Interviews and Other Writings 1972-1977*, translated by Colin Gordon et al., ed. C. Gordon [New York: Pantheon Books, 1980], pp. 81 – 2).

[2] Jacques Derrida, *Of Grammatology*, translated by Gayatri Chakravorty Spivak (Baltimore and London: The Johns Hopkins University Press, 1976), p. 227.

[3] Michel Foucault, "Nietzsche, Genealogy, History", in *The Foucault Reader*, ed. Paul Rabinow (London: Penguin Books, 1991), p. 78.

[4] Judith Butler, *Gender Trouble: Feminism and the Subversion of Identity* (New York and London: Routledge, 1990), p. 143. According to Rosi Braidotti the process of subjection is double: "active (subject of) and passive (subjected to)" (*Patterns of Dissonance. A Study of Women in Contemporary Philosophy*, translated by Elizabeth Guild [1ˢᵗ ed. 1991; Oxford: Polity Press, 1996], p. 48).

diaries and maps) and his hidden but more real life, evokes the notion that the discourses of diaries and maps do not directly represent his experiences but squeeze them into known forms that exclude important aspects. Deconstruction is a critical practice that is effective in undermining the power of such normative representations, which purport to offer the "truth", by showing how they construct meaning through exclusion. Winterson's writing itself is deconstructive: the text undermines the innocence of conventional forms of representation and seeks alternative ways of describing human experiences. Thus Jordan's opposition to traditional ways of representing life (diaries and maps) directs attention to the power and distortion of these discourses. Empowering the inner life of the imagination, the text challenges these outer representations.

In relation to identity there is also convergence between postmodernist theories and Winterson's text. The notion of identity as something that is *not* known to the subject conveys postmodernist perceptions of identity as fundamentally unstable and contradictory. Postmodernists deconstruct the unified and self-knowing subject and replace it by an open and fragmented subject that is perpetually reconstructed; instead of expression, identity is a practice and related to *doing*. One way of illustrating the shift in perception of subjectivity is to argue that postmodernists replace the *cogito* with a *desidero*.[5] Whereas the *cogito* refers to the rational subject with an inner core that may be expressed, the *desidero* relates identity to unconscious desire and in consequence makes it retrospective: we can only know who we are by seeing where we have been or how we have practised our identity. This directs attention to the narratological perception of identity, that it only exists as narrative.[6] This perception has two implications: firstly we have to tell our story in order to tell who we are; secondly we learn how to self-narrate from other stories. Thus narratives have "the potential to teach us how to conceive of ourselves, what to make of our inner life and how to organise it" (Currie, p. 17). Jordan's problem is that existing narratives do not fit his inner life, and the text struggles to narrate a more *real* story of identity.

The deconstruction of identity also affects the perceived relation between body, gender and identity. Instead of seeing sex as the biological foundation of gender, "sex" is a powerful construct in relation to subjection that creates the sexual identities "man" and "woman".[7] In order to emphasise that sex is not the natural core of a gendered identity, the American philosopher Judith Butler

[5] Rosi Braidotti, *Nomadic Subjects. Embodiment and Sexual Difference in Contemporary Feminist Theory* (New York: Columbia University Press, 1994), p. 13.

[6] Mark Currie, *Postmodern Narrative Theory* (London: Macmillan Press LTD, 1998), p. 17.

[7] Michel Foucault, *The History of Sexuality. Volume One: An Introduction*, translated by Robert Hurley (1st ed. 1978; London: Penguin Books, 1990), p. 154.

redefines gender as a "performative practice" (Butler 1990). It is the perpetual re-enactment of gender that creates the *effect* of a natural sexed core of identity that is claimed to be its *cause*. As gender is the mark that humanises the subject, the assumption of gender is necessary, but since sex is not a natural core, gender norms may be recited subversively. Thus Butler relates agency to a resistance to identity instead of seeing identity as the basis of political action. The notion of gender as a performance shall guide my reading of Winterson, as fiction may be a useful medium for subversive gender performances.

In order to give perspective to my reading of *Sexing*, I shall first introduce two of Winterson's other novels, where the theme of identity also prevails. Winterson's first novel *Oranges Are Not the Only Fruit* (1985) is a semi-autobiographic *Bildungsroman* that traces the development of the protagonist "Jeanette". However, *Oranges* is not a conventional *Bildungsroman*, but a postmodernist reworking of the traditional form: the protagonist does not find her place in society, but acknowledges the fundamentally unstable condition of the world. Jeanette handles this instability by telling her own stories—she narrativises her identity. *Written on the Body*, Winterson's fourth novel from 1992, is a postmodernist love story, which struggles to speak of *true* love in the face of romantic clichés. The fascination of this novel is the construction of a narrator that is not clearly gendered, as the narrative voice is not identified as either female or male. Instead of stabilising the narrative position through sexing, the gender position of the narrator is perpetually constructed and deconstructed. Thus while Jeanette in *Oranges* is expelled from her community because her way of *doing* identity does not adhere to the unwritten rules of coherence between sex, gender and sexual orientation,[8] *Written* attempts to do away with sex and gender all together.

In *Sexing*, which is positioned between *Oranges* and *Written*, Winterson explores realms of identity that are bared when the coherent subject or the unified "I" is dismantled. The title of the novel refers to sex as an applicable characteristic ("to give a sex") and the novel may be the link that points toward the radical deconstruction of sex in *Written*. Here I wish to look at how Winterson represents identity in relation to sex and gender in this novel and thereby elaborate the position of *Sexing* and the increasing destabilisation of identity in Winterson's texts. This postmodernist reading is particularly inspired by the work of Michel Foucault and Judith Butler. Following their recommendation of resistance to identity, I shall focus on representations of subjectivity that embody new ways of

---

[8] Jeanette is female (sex); however, she is also a preacher (gender), and in Great Britain this powerful practice is reserved for men *and* Jeanette's mother. Furthermore, Jeanette—in addition to her love for God—loves women (sexual orientation).

thinking about sex and gender and thus push the boundaries of sexual identities.

Sexing is set in the seventeenth and twentieth centuries. Instead of offering a logical and coherent explanation of the exact relation between these epochs, the text questions linear time. The prologue raises doubt about the firmness of the conventional great stabilisers time and matter: there is a sophisticated language without past, present and future tenses; and matter is "mostly empty space" (p. 8). Throughout, the text undermines general perceptions of time and matter as "real" and reinstates them as cultural conventions. The resulting ontological instability is reflected in the fragmentation of the narrative position within the text, which is further complicated by a high level of incorporated stories. *Sexing* is told by four different first-person narrators. The seventeenth-century perspectives are told by the Dog Woman and her adopted son Jordan. At the end of the novel these seventeenth-century narrators are doubled by—or extended into—twentieth-century counterparts: the naval officer Nicolas Jordan and a chemist who camps by a river in her fight against pollution. Shifts in narrative position are not easily distinguished, but they are indicated by drawings as an alternative way of representing characters in a novel. The Dog Woman, who raises dogs for racing and fighting, is represented by the phallic symbol of a banana. When Jordan was a child she took him to see the first banana in England. Jordan, who heroically brings the first pineapple to England, is represented by a pineapple. In the twentieth century Nicholas, who attempts to turn a common pineapple into a rarity, is represented by a cleft pineapple, and the chemist by a banana with one end cut off.

As a young man in the seventeenth century Jordan dreams of becoming a hero. He goes on adventurous quests with the historical hero John Tradescant, who brings back exotic rarities from newly discovered countries. However, in contrast to Tradescant, to whom "being a hero comes naturally", Jordan's style undermines traditional heroism (p. 101). Though they travel together, Jordan's personal journeys are not identical with Tradescant's, whose journeys can be completed and represented in heroic form. The journeys Jordan wishes to tell about are not "real", and in contrast to the meticulous mapping, fixing and categorising that is part of Tradescant's quests, Jordan defies this external form of representation. To Jordan the essential is not found in the material that may be described, but "squashed between the facts" (p. 10). Challenging conventional ways of representation, the purpose of telling his story is not to make log-book records, but to record his journeys with another dimension of "truth": "I've written down my own journey and drawn my own map. I can't show this to the others, but I believe it to be a faithful account of what happened, at least, of what happened to me" (p. 102). Instead of offering a heroic representation of himself, Jordan aims to answer the question "Where are you?" that people ask when he is obviously *absent*.

Jordan is on a quest for identity. Not knowing himself fully he initially suspects that he is running away, but he discovers that he is "running towards": travelling is an "effort to catch up with [his] fleet-footed self, living another life in a different way" (p. 80). However, he realises that the self cannot be captured by representation:

> The self is not contained in any moment or any place, but it is only in the intersection of moment and place that the self might, for a moment, be seen vanishing through a door, which disappears at once (p. 80).

Identity is an unstable "co-ordinate" and may merely be glimpsed (p. 93). Jordan feels that he has lost himself in the "gap between [his] ideal of [him-]self and [his] pounding heart" (p. 101). It is the realisation of the ideal that makes a hero like Tradescant. To Jordan the ego is a "hollow, screaming cadaver that has no spirit within it"; that cadaver is "the ideal self run mad" (p. 103). Rejecting the ego, Jordan's quest does not uncover a unified self. Instead, his effort to describe his inner experiences truthfully bares a multiplicity of elusive selves in fantastic narratives that include cross-gender experiences as he dresses as a woman and lives like one for a while.

In contrast to Jordan's quest for identity, the Dog Woman is firmly situated in the flesh of her material body, and she describes her extraordinary self by more conventional ways of representation. The Dog Woman is of a monstrous size and appearance. She describes herself as a "hill of dung" (p. 11) or a "mountain of ... flesh" (p. 14). Her material existence is emphasised as she uses her immense strength in fights that often end with the death of her adversaries. She claims to be heavier than an elephant *and* that her mother could carry her, implying that material weight matters less than love. Thus the Dog Woman's tale does not purport the material as irrefutable facts but rather as a means of representing: "does it matter if the place cannot be mapped as long as I can still describe it?" (p. 15).

To the Dog Woman the "earth is surely a manageable place made of blood and stone and entirely flat" (p. 23). This comment, apart from demonstrating the Dog Woman's self-sufficiency, illustrates how her matter-of-fact voice represents even stranger visions than Jordan's elusive style. There is a huge contrast between her common-sense attitude and her monstrous actions (murdering her adversaries for a wrong word). She fears that Jordan's lack of common sense will make him follow his dreams till he falls off the (flat) earth, but her own "common sense" is surely not common but rather strange (p. 40).

The Dog Woman purports directly to represent reality as it *is* and she confidently situates events within the conventional, linear calendar. However, her trust in language as directly representing the 'real' is undermined: taking words literally, she misunderstands people, although she can see no wrong done. For example she bites off a man's penis when he asks her to put it in her mouth "as a delicious thing to eat" (p. 41). While these misunderstandings have a humorous effect, they also direct focus to the ambiguity of language and the perpetual deferral of meaning.

In the twentieth century Nicolas Jordan traces his reason for joining the navy back to his childhood dreams of becoming a hero. A hero has a strong self, is self-sufficient and reckless:

> If you're a hero you can be an idiot, behave badly, ruin your personal life, have any number of mistresses and talk about yourself all the time.... Heroes are immune. They have wide shoulders and plenty of hair and wherever they go a crowd gathers. Mostly they enjoy the company of other men, althougt attractive women are part of their reward (pp. 117 - 8).

But like Jordan, Nicolas is not really interested in becoming a hero or in the breaking of world records. In the twentieth century the project of mapping and categorising, initiated in the seventeenth century by explorers like Tradescant, is almost completed. Most things, including the self, can be represented and Nicolas is able to offer a precise description of himself in few words (p. 114). Thus wilderness is disappearing and the entire universe is soon *known*. However, Nicolas is aware that he can only describe himself on the outside, and surface representation of matter, including himself, does not extinguish the magic of his experiences. As Nicolas discovers the blackness "squashed between the facts", he feels as if he falls "into a black hole with no stars and no life and no helmet" (p. 121). Thus Nicolas discovers hidden doors between the "facts".

As Nicolas reads about the chemist's demonstration by a river, he changes his perception of heroism: "Surely this woman was a hero? Heroes give up what's comfortable in order to protect what they believe in or to live dangerously for the common good" (p. 138). Learning that the chemist is persecuted instead of recognised, Nicolas sets out to find her.

The chemist has been alone for a long time and though she has a watch and calendar and is able to situate herself within linear time, her personal experience of time is taking over: "my strongest instinct is to abandon the common-sense approach and accept what is actually happening to me; that time has slowed down" (p. 126). This woman may be linked with the Dog Woman: "I am a woman going mad. I am a woman hallucinating. I imagine I am huge, raw, a giant" (p. 121). She complains that there is "no Rabelaisian dimension for rage", but the Dog Woman in the seventeenth century may be a projection of her rage—her monstrous *alter ego* (p. 124). The chemist has lost patience with the apathy of the world around her and imagines extreme methods for changing it by enforced feminism and ecology.

Letting go of time, the chemist's self becomes fluent: though outwardly she sits by a rotting river, inwardly she is not always present. She escapes the foreground of experiences fixed in time to explore what is forced into the background. Thus, like Nicolas, she traces her life between the "facts" of time and matter. The chemist does not think of identity as unified, but multiple, and with a dimension of space rather than confinement. She uses mercury as a metaphor for identity: "Drop it and it shivers in clones of itself all over the floor, but you can scoop it up again and there won't be any seams or shatter marks. It's one life or countless lives *depending on what you want*" (p. 126, emphasis added). Identity depends upon perception—what is foregrounded and what is backgrounded.

To the chemist, who was overweight as a child, fat is "one of the mysteries of matter": it appears and disappears. Furthermore, it is matter that matters in different ways:

> When the weight had gone I found out something strange: that the weight persisted in my mind. I had an *alter ego* who was huge and powerful, a woman whose only morality was her own and whose loyalties were fierce and few (p. 125).

This powerful *alter ego* empowers the fight against pollution in a world where her work is scorned and her results discredited. Pollution research is not popular: people will not believe the truth, and governments are not interested in research that connects pollution with profitable companies. However, the chemist can no longer keep her monstrous dimensions in the background. She has "lost patience with this hypocritical stinking world", and driven by the passivity of others she is prepared to go to extremes (p. 127). When Nicolas finds her, she suggests that they burn down the polluting factory. Simultaneously (!) the Dog Woman encourages the fire of London in the seventeenth century. Thus fire connects the two epochs at the end of the novel. Having "done with this time and place", the Dog Woman and Jordan escape burning London and sail towards the sea (p. 143).

Sexing explores different ways of understanding time and materiality—and stresses the interrelatedness of these co-ordinates in relation to identity. By undermining time and matter as stable, identity is radically destabilised. Thus Winterson's text is characterised by an inherent ontological instability that reflects postmodernist theories. Through the fragmentation of the narrative viewpoint, the text explores different ways of understanding and representing identity. In this vein the text challenges the traditional realistic representation of diaries and maps and emphasises the power of the imagination in the individual's grasp on reality. Identity is not rooted in an essential core, but related to individual perceptions. Especially the Dog Woman's viewpoint is strange, but Jordan's stories also question ordinary "facts" in regard to the nature of identity, time and matter.

The postmodernist perception of a fundamentally unstable character of existence affects both plot and identity. I think these two entities are connected in literature; the destabilisation of one affects the other. However, I do not mean to imply that one of these is primary and thus causes disruption in the other. A narratological approach highlights the interrelation between plot and identity; identity as narrative means that it depends upon available plots. The plot of *Sexing*, like the narrative voice, is fragmented and the text tells several independent stories. These stories are narrative illustrations of postmodernist destabilisation. For example Jordan's story of a place where language is more material than the body illustrates the postmodernist argument about the materiality of discourse. Thus plot (as coherent progress of events) is deferred in order to pursue a subject matter and represent the world anew. Plot may be compared to Foucault's notion of meta-theories; that is, like universal theories, plot obscures the "subjugated" knowledges of the inconsistencies and contradictions that characterise experiences. As a kind of genealogical writing, Winterson's text breaks the established "truth" and reinstates "countermemories" (Foucault 1980 and 1991). Winterson's genealogical fiction focuses upon inconsistencies of experience and undermines meta-narratives of progress and coherence. Thus genealogical writing uncovers the power implicated in construction and allows excluded experiences to return.

The subversion of plot and the rejection of temporal causality affect the representations of fictional characters. Winterson's characters are not essentialised subjects, but subject positions whence existence may be perceived. Narrators often refer to the impossibility of knowing their own selves, suspecting hidden motives behind their own actions. They resemble the postmodernist subject that does not know itself fully (*desidero*). I think the trouble of defining the position of the narrators within the text reflects this perception of identity: the non-unified perspective is a consequence of the postmodernist destabilisation of identity, as the perceiving subject is not a coherent, meaning-generating entity. The use of fruit symbols to indicate who is speaking emphasises the element of construction involved.

The art of grafting offers a way of understanding the relations between the different narrators: they are grafted onto the author.

> Grafting is the means whereby a plant, perhaps tender or uncertain, is fused into a hardier member of its strain, and so the two take advantage of each other and produce a third kind, without seed or parent (p. 78).

The different voices are fused into the author's voice to make a "hardier" narrative without referring to the author as parent and final referent of the text.[9] Grafting in relation to humans is suggested by Jordan's wish to graft some of Tradescant's hero qualities onto himself and the Dog Woman's objection to this "unnatural" practice: "Thou mayest as well try to make a union between thyself and me by sewing us at the hip" (79). Through the metaphor of grafting, Winterson represents identity as radically fragmented and multiple—and in consequence dependent upon construction. Also she emphasises that the same subject unproblematically lives with opposing principles. With regard to identity, the subject may have one self or multiple selves. Identity is both unified and fluent. By shifting between different narrative positions, Winterson explores these different perceptions of identity. However, each of the narrators also deconstructs any coherent perception of their own identity. For example the substantial Dog Woman can melt into the night and weighs nothing in water.

The destabilisation of the perceiving subject also affects the application of conventional gender norms. The deconstruction of a natural link between sex and gender is foregrounded by the fruit symbols: the phallic banana represents the two female narrators while the pineapple represents the male ones. Furthermore, the characters unproblematically cross conventional gender boundaries and these crossings appear unremarkable. Sex does not limit the textual performance of gender. Instead both sex and gender are denaturalised—like time and matter, neither sex nor gender is a stable characteristic of identity. This is suggested by

---

[9] I here draw upon Roland Barthes' renowned essay "The Death of the Author" (*Image Music Text*, selected and translated by Stephen Heath [London: Fontana Press, 1977]). In declaring the death of the "Author-God" (p. 146), Barthes terminates the representational view of literary language. Instead of seeing the author as the final signified that explains a text, Barthes claims that "Writing is that neutral, composite, oblique space where our subject slips away, the negative where all identity is lost, starting with the very identity of the body writing" (p. 142).

the title; "sexing" refers to sex, not as a natural given, but as an applied characteristic. It is further elaborated in the botanical technique of grafting, which Jordan applies to the cherry tree. The Dog Woman questions the sex of the tree Jordan is creating, calling it a monster. As Jordan explains that the cherry will be sexed, she says that "such things ha[ve] no gender and [are] a confusion to themselves" (p. 79). Thus the Dog Woman, herself a monster unlimited by gender convention, insists on sex as the characteristic that makes plants as well as humans intelligible.[10] Though her name indicates her sex, the Dog Woman's power, like the chemist's anger, diverges from acceptable norms of femininity. Thus while sex is applicable to the characters of the novel, in order not to make them "a confusion to themselves", it is not a determining characteristic. The flexible and multiple selves deconstruct stabilised sexual identities. Both Jordan and the Dog Woman are unconstrained by conventional gender norms as the Dog Woman's impressive size and force exceeds any human norms, and Jordan cross-dresses (both literally and metaphorically). On his "journeys", Jordan meets people burdened by gender, but his powerful imagination enables him to escape the heavy burden of gender norms. In the twentieth century both the chemist and Nicolas are expected to adhere to the gender norms that are related to their sex: Nicolas is expected to be ambitious and heroic while the chemist is advised to abandon her aggressive political project, and smile, marry and "do worthy work behind the scenes" (p. 125). Identity as narrative may explain the function of the seventieth century narrators: they are Nicolas' and the chemist's attempt to escape the restricting norms of their culture by narrativising their lives and thus tell who they *really* are—or their experienced identity. Thus the monstrous Dog Woman may be "the chemist's other life, a narrativisation of something which is lacking in her real(ized) identity".[11] Just as the Dog Woman gives the chemist a power for action, Jordan allows Nicolas to put his inner journeys into discourse and explore the blackness between the facts. By deconstructing the masculine heroic form, Nicolas narrativises personal experiences that are not limited by his sex (or the masculine ego), but include feelings that belong to both sides of the gender dichotomy.

Though Winterson represents subjects as fragmented and without any essential foundation, *Sexing* still represents a character who performs politically: the chemist effectuates her resistance against pollution. The chemist's fight against pollution is a strategy of resistance and the fight over the right to define the truth of mercury levels in rivers and lakes illustrates the problem of taking action when truth is

---

[10] Though Foucault and Butler deconstruct "sex" they agree that sex humanises the subject: in order to be recognised as human one must have a sex (Foucault 1990, pp. 155 - 6 and Butler 1990, p. 111).
[11] Marianne Børch, "Jeanette Winterson", *ANGLOfiles*, 100 (February 1997), p. 66.

related to power: the chemist's facts are countered by polluting companies and governments that defend their policy. However, when identity is perceived as an effect of doing, the unified subject is not a precondition for action—like Butler's claim that agency does not depend upon the essentialised subject.[12] *Sexing* replaces the traditionally celebrated and unified hero—who is just as reckless as the angry chemist—by the fragmented subject. By reformulating heroism from a way of being to a way of doing, the text represents a *doer*, who, like the Dog Woman, "cares nothing for how she looks, only for what she does" (p. 101). In burning down the factory the chemist lives out her imagined identity as a monster, and through this performance it has political consequences (Børch, p. 66). A monster signifies resistance to identity, as monsters cross boundaries of the unified subject. Thus this grafted agent illustrates that agency depends upon construction—not "identity".

In *Gender Trouble*, Judith Butler claims that as "trouble", over meanings of gender, is inevitable, the task is how best to make it (p. vii). According to my reading, Winterson makes gender trouble in her texts by destabilising the "facts" of both gender and sex in relation to identity. Perhaps the artist holds a more privileged position than the philosopher and theorist in regard to rewriting the body and giving expression to personal experiences within postmodernist discourse. Whereas postmodernist critics often refrain from working directly with the body (in spite of the ambition to incorporate the materiality of the body in theoretical discourse) due to a common dread of essentialism, fiction writers narrativise personal experiences. Gender trouble is evident in Winterson's novels. *Oranges* emphasises individual problems of adhering to culturally imposed gender norms that are expected to give expression to biological sex. In *Sexing* conventional gender connotations are perpetually violated, and sex is referred to as an ascribed characteristic—a cultural construct that regulates individuals. Thus the grafting and sexing in *Sexing* prepares the subversive performances of the narrator in *Written* that disrupt any coherence between body, gender and identity. While *Sexing* mobilises gender categories and refers to sex as an organising principle, *Written* uses gender connotations to describe human experiences of love without stabilising these by sex.

The contemporary questioning of the unified subject is clearly embodied in Winterson's texts. In *Sexing*, Jordan abandons the search for a unified identity

---

[12] Butler discusses the necessary redefinition of agency *from* traditional identity politics, where it is based upon a stable and preexisting subject, *to* understanding agency without "a doer behind the deed". Agency is simply a variation on the necessary repetition of the "rules that govern intelligible identity" (pp. 142, 145).

and the chemist lets her multiple selves loose. The novel does not lament the loss of "identity", but shows how too much ego restricts the subject. In this vein, the traditional heroic form is countered by stories that depict the vigourous experiences that we may recognise when we look beyond the limiting ego. Thus Winterson's novel shows the multiple possibilities of a fragmented subjectivity. In the collection of essays *Art Objects* Winterson describes the function of *true* art thus: "*art is pushing at the boundaries we thought were fixed*" (p. 116, emphasis added). In relation to sexual identities, Winterson's subversive fiction may push the boundaries of gendered identities to prove them less fixed than we think. If we dare trust the transformative power of art, we may read Winterson's texts as explorations of identity that empower our multiple selves to become grafted agents.

Love's Ontology and the Problem of Cliché
by Marianne Børch

for Peggy Reynolds with love
(*Written on the Body*, dedication)

If I am in love with Peggy and ... I am a writer, I ... must not fall
into the trap of believing that my passion, of itself, is art .... I know
that I shall have to find a translation of form to make myself clear.
I know that the language of my passion and the language of my art
are not the same thing (*Art Objects*, p. 105).

In *Boating for Beginners* the heroine, Gloria Munde, dreams of an eagle erupting
out of her stomach to pick her up and carry her to the top of a bright, slippery
mountain. An orange demon asks her, "Did you grow out of the eagle or did the
eagle grow out of you?" (p. 74). The episode recalls two crucial moments in the
formation of the European tradition of vernacular poetry, vizz. Dante's *Divina
Commedia* and Chaucer's *House of Fame* (*HF*). In the *Commedia*, Dante, in quest
of saving illumination, interiorises his exemplar and guide, the classical poet Virgil.
In *HF*, Chaucer, directly responding to Dante's passage, has his alter ego convert
an eagle, like Virgil a near-metonymy of an intellectual artistic tradition, from
domineering obstacle into obedient vehicle, suggesting how tradition is
subordinated to, and integrated within, the author's poetic. With such symbolically
resonant imagery and famous intertexts and the question asked by the "genius" of

a person named "Light of the World", the eagle in *Boating* clearly raises the question of the poet's relation to tradition to suggest that a poet is born through strong misprision of a beloved, but potentially oppressive tradition.[1] Moreover, tradition seems for the poets both old and new to pose similar problems and lead to similar choices. Chaucer and Dante, faced with an authoritative Latin tradition, redeploy and refashion genres from a popular tradition excluded from official authority, notably the romance; choose for their greatest ventures the vernacular; and use a tradition of secular love poetry to explore the highest metaphysical questions. Winterson, too, experiences a conflict between an elitist canon and a marginalised tradition, and chooses the romance, still a genre of doubtful authority, to make it the site for contesting—whilst refusing to replace—the authority of an institutionally sanctified male-fostered canon;[2] furthermore, like her fourteenth-century forebears, Winterson uses human love as the tool that will wrench open an epistemology giving at the seams, and like Chaucer especially, she identifies, and explores the consequences of, the failure of human discourse and social codes to accommodate desire.

While her stance of deliberately decentred authority logically leads to romance (always the "secular scripture"[3]), Winterson like Chaucer and Dante monitors, and guards against, its inherent dangers. Chaucer used romance to problematise both its form and its epistemological tenets; Dante, claiming the authority of the allegedly trivial, raised romance by making it the vehicle of a cognitive quest.[4] Romance raises similar self-consciousness in contributors to its modern revival, as these take up a genre nearly extinct,[5] though quietly pursuing its own life in the "consumer literature" of weeklies and newsstand novels. In *Oranges*, Winterson exposes sentimental romance as a strategy for promoting God or heterosexual marriage; in *Boating*, it is caricatured in the figure and effusions of Bunny Mix, while narrator and characters dissect and denounce its demagogic-somatic potential. In *Written on the Body*, however, Winterson confronts the fact that, like the old masters, she needs that popular tradition, although, also like them, she *needs it with a difference*. Whilst problematising romance's characteristic idiom, she embraces its epistemological and ethical value

---

[1] In line with the theory of Harold Bloom, *The Anxiety of Influence* (Oxford: Oxford University Press, 1973/1997).

[2] *ArtOb*, p. 61.

[3] Implications explored in Northrop Frye's book of that name, (Cambridge, Mass.: Harvard University Press, 1979).

[4] For Chaucer, study "Sir Thopas" (style); "Knight's Tale", "Franklin's Tale", *Troilus & Criseyde* (epistemology). For Dante's defence of vernacular and romance, see *De Vulgari Eloquentia*, I, 16; II, 2, 4.

[5] Writing just before romance's new boom, Gillian Beer, in *The Romance* (London: Methuen, 1970), depicts realism's progress at the cost of romance.

and ponders the enigma that this tritest of generic clichés still seems ideal for authentic and innovative expression.

Poststructuralist terminology will occasionally appear in the following, but arguably the best set of tools for examining her text is a pattern of concepts, themes, and tropes in *Written* itself which refers back precisely to the medieval tradition of self-conscious love romance. Here Winterson finds a resource for filling verbal gaps in today's lexicon which show that love has lost its cognitive credibility. Love lingers on in modern discourse as clichés done to death by repetition: "I love you"; or in idioms emptied of semantic content by Enlightenment scepticism.

> You had no choice, you were swept away. Forces took you and possessed you .... In the late twentieth century we still look to ancient demons to explain our commonest action (*Written*, p. 39).

The failure of love to generate new discourse shows that even as God is excluded from Frye's "third-phase" discourse, so is love.[6] In the medieval tradition, however, Winterson finds a problematisation of love conducted within an epistemology for which Love is metonymical with God. Continuing its critical inquiry, Winterson wields the tradition as a weapon against an epistemology that makes invisible and wordless experience that demands to be seen and spoken, protesting the need for new, serious discourse of love. Not surprisingly, Winterson, in redeploying clichés of genre and idiom, serves that noble cause herself: in *Written*, Winterson, like her predecessors in the same plight, forces *her* founding fathers to bless her in a wrestling match of radical creative misprision.[7]

Among Winterson's works, *Written on the Body* is that which makes fewest incursions into the realm of the fantastic. The single wild card in the book is the undeclared sex of the main character; otherwise, the book depicts the classical triangle of man, wife, and lover, a cliché so common that it can be summed up in a miniature drama, whose script is duly provided (pp. 14 - 5). The plot proceeds in a relatively straight line as the memoir of a single narrator. Brief bursts of fantastic narrative are anchored in the main narrative as easily identifiable

---

[6] Northrop Frye, *The Great Code* (London: Routledge and Kegan Paul, 1981), pp. 15 - 18.

[7] The following analysis of Bloomesque misprision has implications for the ongoing debate, discussed by Kim L. Worthington in *Self as Narrative* (Oxford: Clarendon Press, 1996), about the possibility of "personal authenticity and subjective agency" (Worthington, p. 8). Identified as a function of language, an authentic, autonomous self is often denied in poststructuralist accounts, or deemed possible only in the form of (Lyotardesque) liberating madness. Winterson could be said to support the case for "'rule-bound' deviance" (p. 11), "the possibility of narrative creativity within communicative protocols and ... transformative possibilities of creative self-narration" (p. 18).

explorations of the madness or erotic transport of the protagonist; even a distinct oddity, an anatomical prose poem interrupting the main narrative, is clearly identified as a "love-poem" (p. 111), which accounts for its metaphorical and other peculiarities.

The one recognisable feature from Winterson's earlier books is the use of the repeated phrase or recurrent, symbolically significant object. "It's the clichés that cause the trouble" and "I love you", spoken by the narrator, and "I'll never let you go", spoken by the heroine Louise, exemplify the former type of repetition; a series of armchairs, the latter.

Clichés are themselves a comfortable armchair longed for by the protagonist at the opening of the book (p. 10), and later one rather defeatedly acknowledged as a possible ending (p. 188); a real armchair figures in a vision of the disconsolate lover withering away to dust (pp. 107 - 8), a tragic situation which is nevertheless deliberately chosen, as was the armchair life with the lover's girlfriend, Jacqueline (p. 26).

If Jacqueline's armchair suggests a life stuck in clichés, the protagonist chooses this to escape from an even bigger cliché masquerading as freedom: the life of a quasi-professional lover exchanging partners with clockwork regularity. Many of the lover's previous adventures are recounted in flashbacks, where they offer not only comic relief from the painful intensity of the central love story, but also multiple perspectives upon love in a quasi-typological pattern that cuts across the linear plot. "No-one can legislate love" (p. 77) is the exuberant legitimising mantra of the lover's life. However, almost from the beginning, the lover's freedom is exposed as pseudo-freedom: illegitimacy confines the lovers to small, secret spaces, and the lover becomes Caliban, locked in an alien language (see below, p. 10). The compensation for the social and linguistic exclusion from the public domain—the champagne, midnight telephone calls and spontaneous flights—really entail sameness without a difference, and repetition brings on a parabolic extenuation which no escalation or excess will remedy: in the end, the champagne is served up by Boredom, the very Butler who first gave access to the married mistress (p. 15). Paradoxically, the one thing such truant love cannot accommodate, is love: the scripted sketch shows the lover crying, unseen and separate from the adoring mistress (p. 15).

The heroine Louise breaks the vicious circle of the lover's going from one cliché to the other, from "slop-bucket of romance" to armchair. However, when Louise is found to have cancer and the lover renounces her into the arms of her cancer expert husband, heroic self-sacrifice is exposed as yet another selfish cliché. While the armchair passage (pp. 107 - 8) is a lyrical master-piece, its tragic pathos is yet modified, not only by the symbolic link between armchair and cliché, but also by the echo of a previous scene of mourning the loss of Louise. Expecting to be abandoned, the distraught lover develops a fever, then turns delirious—"with luck, I might even die" (p. 95), and a bottle of gin does the rest. Louise rescues the lover from this pitiful farce. But there is yet another, yet earlier, analogue which shows the same routine enacted, and with a different woman (p. 44). Identifying the element of habit in the final crisis, the two earlier episodes proleptically interpret the defeatist pathos of the armchair, overlaying the lover's self-sacrifice with narcissistic implications ("nothing so sweet as wallowing in it" [p. 26]), and foregrounding a suggestion that renunciation, far from expressing love, excludes it in a regression to the six-month cycle. However, Louise once again saves the protagonist from behavioral cliché (whether literally or symbolically), though arguably in a manner that triggers another grand cliché: Louise is the one and only, love conquers all, no cost is too high, no pain too deep: "Love is worth it" (p. 156).

Throughout, *Written* balances precariously on the edge of cliché, acknowledging its value and yet complaining: "It's the clichés that cause the trouble" (pp. 10, 21, 26, 71, 155, 180). Clichés appear in multiple manifestations: as verbal cliché ("I love you"), generic cliché (romance), codes of behaviour (the secret meeting, marriage), specialised idioms (traditional love poetry, medical jargon), and ontological norms (constructions of sexuality and individuality). Winterson, in fact, makes an exploration of the enigma of cliché—the very essence of repetition, yet spontaneously used to enunciate uniqueness—the road to clarifying love's ontology. In *Written*, she shows how clichés destroy the love they are often invoked to express, and identifies the cause: cliché is prior to individual usage, repetition and iterability being the conditions of its recognisability and use; love, however, is unique.

Conventional scripts bring armchair comfort. The lover is a great writer of scripts, a craft perfected through constant exercise, as when (s)he makes up speeches for people seen through windows (p. 59), pens the above-mentioned play, and stages secret meetings for momentary enjoyment of freedom from marital bondage. Scripts are the lover's weapon against uncertainty—including that brought on by love. Love is Alice in Wonderland (p. 10), unfamiliar territory regulated by forces the lover "can't quantify or contain", but can only register by its effect, utter confusion (p. 53). Even the desired event of Louise choosing the lover beyond the wonted six months is felt to be "the wrong script" (p. 56). Throughout, love is evoked in imagery of invasion, burning, scorching, and cutting. Louise is a Gothic heroine with a burning bush of red hair, uncanny in her intensity and disregard of common sense, a volcano likely to carbonise her lover Pompeii (p. 49); "beneath her control there was a crackling power of the kind that makes me nervous when

I pass pylons" (p. 49), an energy which at one point nearly electrocutes the lover (p. 36), used to thinking of changing mistresses as discardable batteries for recharging "those fading cells" (p. 76).

Yet destruction marks a step towards reconstruction: what love burns away is the old personality—an identity constituted through a repetition of identical conquests ("scalps", p. 53). Louise demands that the lover come to her "without a past ... new" (p. 54), and soon the lover's past is consumed in delirious dreams (p. 69), leaving a "space uncluttered by association" (p. 81):

> Under her fierce gaze my past is burned away. The beloved as nitric acid. Am I hoping for a saviour in Louise? An almighty scouring of deed and misdeed leaving the slab clean and white? (p.77).

The apocalyptic imagery suggests an identity radically "made new" by Louise, who looks at the lover the way God looked at Adam (p. 18); and rewrites a body palimpsestically overlaid with old texts (pp. 89, 106). Love's transfiguration encompasses all things, dissolving boundaries between subject and object: infused with her presence, Louise's kitchen is a "code ... to crack" (p. 50), her soup endowed with sacramental power (pp. 49 - 50), her touch enough to release from a simple pear centuries of history (p. 37). Paths all leading to Louise spring up in a complex manuscript illumination, a painted wilderness, tea leaves in a cup. Louise transforms not only space, but also time: "Who are you for whom time has no meaning", ponders the lover, who swears to love Louise beyond time, even beyond the decay of her body (p. 51).

The reconstructed identity is made out of two souls: Louise is "Déja vu", the lover's "twin" (p. 163): "When I look in the mirror it's not my own face I see. Your body is twice. Once you once me. Can I be sure which is which?" (p. 99).

Fulfilled love is "recognition" between people "familiar", like happily married partners who have "become one another without losing their very individual selves" (p. 82). Imagery describing love's fulfilment collapses categories of child and lover (pp. 80, 81, 91), slippers and dancing-shoes (pp. 71, 79, 81), hearth and quest, virgin and roué (p. 81), even as the "tame domestic space" suddenly turns into a jungle (pp. 68, 73).

The sameness of lover and beloved has been seen as one of the identifying marks of the lover as female, an identification used, first, to account for the prominence of the topos of risk in Winterson's novels, second, to construct out of the alignment same-sex love and risk a lesbian poetic.[8] However, determining the

___

[8] Carolyn Allen, *Following Djuna* (Bloomington: Indiana University Press, 1996). For a discussion

protagonist's sex as female, or male for that matter, arguably works against the text. In *The Passion*, Winterson depicts "playful" uncertainty about gender as the essence of erotic pleasure, play's significance overriding whatever "reality" it hides. In *Written*, as will be seen, she makes such play her theme at all levels, critiquing the merely supplementary, "enhancing", value of play, whilst celebrating play's radically destabilising effect. Thus, with respect to identity, play is the crucial factor in establishing the lover's new identity by which the literally ego-centric personality pushes outward the boundary of the self so as to encompass the beloved. There is no known social, verbal or biological taxonomy for this mysterious construct, although it may be held within the impossible equation of $1+1=1$.[9]

Apocalyptic imagery, the dissolution of boundaries (temporal, spatial, biological, social and logical), and love's radically defamiliarising effect upon experience, point to love's ontologically complex relation to the world of empirical and social reality. Winterson further explores the strangely subversive quality of love by a sinister, and consistently upheld, analogue between love and illness in general, and cancer in particular.

Space allows only a partial account of the complex role played by cancer in *Written*. Introducing cancer into her love story both literally and metaphorically, Winterson basically strengthens the link between love and risk already explored in *The Passion*.[10] First, love is a cancer,[11] a symbolic identification which inverts the lover's automatically negative associations of cancer at the diegetic level. Yet even there cancer suggests value: Louise in an unhappy marriage is sick with cancer of the blood, indicating a deficiency disease—sick *for* love, sick *with* longing for completion in the other; similarly, the lover, previously contaminated with emotional, though not physical "clap" (p. 25), is seen repeatedly and progressively pining away for Louise, until embracing the healthy madness of the final union.

---

of the lover's undeclared sex, see Ute Kauer, "Narration and Gender: The Role of the First-Person Narrator in *Written on the Body*", in *'I'm Telling you Stories': Jeanette Winterson and the Politics of Reading*, eds. Helena Grice and Tim Woods (Amsterdam and Atlanta: Rodopi, 1998), pp. 41 - 52. For lesbian readings, see Louise Horskjær Humphries's article in the present volume.

[9] See David Sinkinson's article "Shadows, signs, wonders ..." for the ontology of this.

[10] See for a brilliant account of this aspect, Carolyn Allen (n. 8), pp. 49 ff.

[11] The analogue love-as-cancer sprouts multiple comparisons. Beyond the ones noted in the text: no one knows why love or cancer strikes or how to cure it (pp. 67/96); neither can be controlled, but only known from its effect (pp. 53/105); normal rules of existence are suspended (pp. 115, 10); the sick body hurts easily, even as intense love-making leaves the heedlessly passionate lover bruised (pp. 39/124); even as the sick body enters a recession of deceptive health (p. 175), so seemingly healthy love may mark a withdrawal into narcissism; cancer invades the body, an intrusion similar to the lover's exploration (pp. 115/123); the cancerous body dances with itself, self intimate with self in the way of dancing lovers (pp. 175/73).

The cure for love-sickness—whole(some)ness through union with the other—is described as a highly risky meeting between compatible molecules; likewise, cancer is possibly cured through proper molecular docking, another high-risk experiment (pp. 61 - 2). Cancer thus suggests break-down, but also potential healing: the body dancing with itself (p. 175) recalls the lovers locked in a lethal, yet inevitably chosen, grip (p. 88). Moreover, by raising the spectre of imminent death, cancer "protects" love, precluding the armchair of habit, and testing a love felt to transcend time, death, and decay (p. 51). The lover fails to pass the test: excluding Louise's body to save her body flouts the necessity conveyed by the imagery of inseparable, death-defying, union; and defers to a definition of individual identity as ego-centric and coalescent with the physical body. However, the lover comes to reaffirm the necessary identity of two-in-one: "This hole in my heart is in the shape of you and no-one else can fit it" (p. 155), acknowledging the validity of an experience inseparable from the flesh, yet also transcending the tragedy of its death.

The lover's previous mistake is traced to an ontological mistake about the place of the body (as representing the material order) in love.

Once united, the lovers spontaneously seek the exclusive space already established through mutual absorption, the six-month-script appearing perfect for the accommodation of desire. The invisibility produced by love—a black hole from which no energy can escape (p. 72), seems indistinguishable from that generated by illegitimacy. Truant love fits true love.

Or not. For although the lover and Louise have no wish to hide their love, they come to experience identical restraints with those for whom isolation and brevity are dictated by social pressure. Even as secret love is sensitive to inquisitive friends and husbands and knocks on the door (pp. 16, 73), so the lovers are unpleasantly conscious of Elgin's peering eyes (p. 98). Similarly, with secrecy follows a semantic reversal of social discourse which isolates lovers as effectively as secrecy itself: early on, Winterson's lover must accept the word "monstrous" for intended honesty with a cuckolded husband (p. 16). With Louise, language is even more intransigent: wishing to break out in tongues of flame (p. 9), the Caliban-savage lover curses a language frustratingly fixed for capturing an essentially elusive experience (pp. 9 - 10), so if clichés make sense to the lover, Adam-new, repetition of "I love you" still produces an "advertising hack" (p. 52). Like people seen through windows like goldfish in a bowl, silently moving their mouths (p. 59), lovers live in a sealed aquarium (p. 72), a "love-lined, lead-lined coffin" (p. 16), emotion sealed up in behavioral code and verbal cliché. No energy can escape, whether exclusive or excluded. "This isn't working", says Louise and changes it. The lover changes it back: "I was lost in my own navigation" (p. 17). Applying past behaviour to a radically new situation, i.e. letting repetition control uniqueness,

the lover moves away from the heroine. Since romance is movement and life,
logically an "anti-quest" spells stasis and death. Louise is elided and caught instead,
by imaginative violence, in a stereotypically perfect image; the lover's heart, dry
and airless, ticks towards standstill (p. 183).[12]

The "vacuum" of that misery is one of the book's many small spaces, the
smallest of which is the world of virtual reality represented by Elgin, the lover's
foil and analogue.

Winterson adopts virtual reality as a metaphor for the secret meetings (pp.
96 - 7) so expertly arranged by the serial lover. Another great manipulator of
reality, however, is Elgin, who, sublimating his grief over his mother's death by
cancer, throws himself into cancer research, but has no place for the body: he sees
no patients, solves his life-and-death problems by trivial computer games, and
has never been seen naked by anyone except Louise. Elgin, encasing human beings
in a computer sarcophagus that removes life before death does, is the apotheosis
of shrunken, yet megalomanic virtuality: $1 \times \infty = 1$.

In the lovers' deadly serious game of "$1+1=1$", however, the body is a
token of exchange, valued, risked—or betrayed. Removing Louise to the virtual
realm of the mind, the lover plays Elgin's game, mimicking the marble man by
donning "shining armour" and excluding Louise's changing body as irrelevant,
the way Elgin avoids contact with patients; Elgin's computer simulations return
in the lover's soap-opera visions of Louise; Elgin removing life prematurely is
duplicated in the lover's premature mourning of Louise, and the lover's
narcissistic withdrawal into morbidity critiqued by its analogy with Elgin's comical
combination of paid-for masochism and inability to connect.

Excluding the vulnerable body, the lover thus plays by rules of the world
for which love is an irrelevance and belongs within the strictly provisional space
of the secret chamber. In fact, the secret meeting may be understood as a reification
of love's emotion, an extension of something basically out of time into a
temporal event, whose brevity, invisibility and "bad fit", however, betray its
impossibility in the physical realm. In this context, the existence of outside
obstacles (Elgin's eyes, the man at the door) are really incidental, actual or projected
manifestations of love's inability to gain physical extension. By accepting a merely
truant script for love, however, lovers accept its provisional, and merely
supplementary, "subworld" status.[13] In so far as social scripts have room for love
as the basis of action at all, it is as a temporary aberrance. And in so far as it is

---

[12] The fading away of the lover's energy is contrapuntally highlighted by a portrait of popular
culture, *itself* engaged in a desperate hunt for value and quality through emersion in gargantuan
quantities of booze, music, and behavioral extravaganzas that mimick springtime renewal.
[13] For the concept of "subworld", see Brian McHale, *Postmodernist Fiction* (London: Routledge,
1989), p. 34.

named or defined, love is labelled madness and best got over. The repetition which defines social and verbal scripts thus excludes the defining features of the emotion they were supposed to express—uniqueness and ("visionary") difference.

At the heart of this near-tragedy, then, lies an epistemological problem: love is virtual, or invisible, not because it is illegitimate, but because it belongs to a different order of experience than the material order. Love is a "heterocosm", superimposed upon the material world and with a necessarily oblique relation to empirical scripts. Occupying parallel planes, the heterocosm and the "real" may share features with "'dual referential allegiance'".[14] Such dual reference may lead to confusing what are in fact dissimilar phenomena, and each determined by its own ontological logic. The secret space may equally denote illegitimacy and intimacy, truancy and truth, exclusion and exclusiveness. In this context, the body is particularly vulnerable to misconstruction, belonging to the material order whilst bringing "recognition" of a world beyond time and space. Acknowledging the difference is nevertheless crucial. Mistaking the truant for the true, love may get trapped in scripts adopted as objective correlatives of love, but in fact created by an outside world to contain it as illegitimate, a supplement that merely consolidates the norm it purports to transcend. Acknowledging the difference, however, opens for recognition that love's qualitative transformation—experienced as all-encompassing—should not be limited to the cycle of truancy. You cannot "legislate love" (p. 77); but you can choose it.

Excluded from repetition, however, love can neither be lived nor spoken—the cliché may feel new, but such renewal cannot carry across the rim of the black hole created by internal fusion. Yet love demands to break through the walls of the aquarium and enter the real and legitimate; this can happen only through an accommodation between old scripts and new vision. Louise knows and shows how to do it. Like the lover a writer of scripts, she shapes hers to serve *her* mantra, "I will never let you go". Her plots, moreover, although determined and scrupulously planned, emulate the mercurial quality of love itself: deriding the sham freedom of clandestine love that will write her into cliché, excluding her "never", she captures her lover ("a game in [her] head" [p. 84]) through a staged, erotically thrilling, "accidental" encounter, a replay of Emma Hamilton's ploy to capture Nelson. To achieve permanence, then, Gothically uncanny Louise thus cultivates fluidity, theatricality, playfulness. Her game issues in yet more play with convention—marriage with a difference, or "marriage", risky in being unprotected by social sanction, sustained by "true minds" alone. The new has been vindicated by reinscription in the old, the old playfully renewed. But how about words?

---

[14] The term is from Benjamin Hrushovski, "Fictionality and frames of reference: remarks on a theoretical framework", *Poetics Today* 5 (1984/2), pp. 227 - 251. Cited in McHale, pp. 27 - 9.

The lover's road back to Louise is mediated by a series of mythical helpers and guides, reminiscent of the fairy tale guides or psychopomps of visionary quests—Chaucer's Eagle, Dante's Virgil, Winterson's orange demons. First, a tempest-tossed cat, soon symbolically named Hopeful, dispells the lover's apathy, as (s)he takes "it by the scruff of the neck the way Louise had taken me" (p. 109). The day after, the lover discards (mere) translation to study medical books and finds there a love-poem (p. 111), a translation of dispassionate medical clichés "in the mode of Louise", a process by which Louise, previously found in objects, landscapes, even the lover's own body, is also finally inscribing herself into language. Louise's entry into the lover's linguistic order enables the lover to respond to a small and growing inner voice (p. 153) seconded by the weirdest, though quite self-conscious of psychopomps, the bar-owner Gail Right:

> " ... What right has [Gail] to poke her nose in your shining armour?
> That's what you're thinking, isn't it, honey? I may not look much
> like a messenger from the gods, but your girl isn't the only one
> who's got wings" (p. 160).

Gail Right is not a giant genie out of a bottle (like Dog Woman in *Sexing the Cherry*), but still monstrously oversized; nor is she an orange demon (as in *Oranges are not the Only Fruit*), but she *is* depicted in orange-striped glory brought on by water from an overworked water-heater stirring up the "sediment"—a substance of mythical uncanniness which comically evokes the lover's stagnant, previously unplumbed depths. And she correctly identifies the lover's heroics as false, pronouncing what the inner voice suggests: wanting to "live in a novel", the lover has, if not invented Louise, then in fact "tried to" (p. 189). The lover's clichés have garbled the true text written by Louise, which was a story of difference, and so, difficulty.

It is nature, throughout the objective correlative of the lover's dessication, that points to imminent change, and that even from the very first page, when "Trees are prospecting underground, sending reserves of roots into the dry ground, roots like razors to open any artery water-fat" (p. 9).[15] The arteries recall a passage on the literally painful intensity of love-making, which for a leukemia patient means plum-purple bruises (p. 124), whereas the razor image anticipates descriptions of desire for Louise's body (p. 131). The imagery of painful natural revival suggests the violence involved in the erasure and reconstruction of identity necessary for the self-consciousness of choice and words; and as so often, Winterson supplements intensity with the epiphanous comedy of a past affair;

---

[15] An echo from Longinus' *De Rerum Naturae* V, ll. 805 - 15.

when former lover Carlo met Roberto, the two "exchanged razorblades and cut me out" (p. 143). How's that for an exemplum of inevitability?

Pain, however, uncovers hidden forces: first, the cleansing "bath night in Yorkshire" provoked by Hopeful (p. 109); then, the comical herald of change by water, the stirred-up orange sediment in the water-tank; finally, the apotheosis of water's return to nature. The regretful lover, returning from a failed attempt to find Louise, plods through a landscape brought back to life at last, a virtual water-world of seeping, trickling, slushing humidity slowly penetrating the drought-dessicated soil (p. 185). The lover's "vital aquafers", likewise, are opening up, ready for recognition of the knowledge suppressed by his own plots.

The love-poem attempts to embrace everything that is Louise. Medical jargon, itself a muffling blanket protecting against pain, a cliché though of an unusual kind, enables the lover to penetrate to the beloved (p. 132). Still, if medical terminology provides the defamiliarising discourse which allows for disinterested contemplation of the intimately known, the passage also suggests that poetic celebration may betray its referent: the celebration grows out of "living on memories" and makes for a bad reproduction of the beloved's actual, decaying self (pp. 124 - 5)—a beautiful lie, in other words, a classical definition of art. This, too, is a coffin, Louise being embalmed in a verbal mausoleum, caught in a photograph (p. 119). The passage, then, ponders the ancient paradox—the way art refines experience, but kills it in the act: still life is still not life.[16] Out there is Louise, ignored like the lady of romances and Petrarchan lyrics, who is star, guiding light and beacon—and utterly irrelevant. The artist betrays the beloved in praising the beloved who inspired the song.

Still, the poem is different from the beautifying fantasy of the armchair: the monument acknowledges its lie, as it acknowledges change; always returning to the hard facts of the human body with all its sordid biological functions, the lover walks the tightrope of the creative act, wresting value from contingency even in transforming it into permanence.

Written thus problematises, but validates, art's transformation of flesh into word. It also illustrates the solution to the problem of speaking the old with a redeeming difference. Even as love breaks the simple division of man into private and social identity, inserting a third intermediary identity ("marriage" spanning gap between institution and emotion), thus love rewrites language "in the mode of Louise", i.e. infusing the common discourse of clichés (trope, idiom, genre, tradition) with personal experience. Where the misprised social code needs inverted commas, renewed discourse has its own word: poetry.

---

[16]   The topos of art and contingency recurs throughout Winterson's oeuvre in meditations on e.g. Keats' "Ode on a Grecian Urn", Eliot's *Four Quartets*, Yeats' "Byzantium", Shakespeare's "Full Fathom Five"; see also, McHale (n.13), p. 230.

As mentioned, *Written* invokes a tradition of texts going back at least to Chaucer's problematisation of Courtly Love in his tragic romances, where lovers discover the meaning of "no-one can legislate love" ("who shal yeve a lovere any lawe", *Knight's Tale*, l. 1164) as they adopt a convention of secret, exclusive love, seemingly ideal for the expression of their emotions, but incompatible with other social scripts, and in the end with love itself; texts, then, which make precisely the tragedy of slavishly following convention the trope of failing to speak the old with seriously playful difference.[17]

While the concept of Courtly Love has tended to be reified and hence dismissed by critics,[18] Winterson grasps it perfectly, not only correcting reifying readings, but herself innovating it in an act of virtuoso "misprision". The complex expansion of the trope of love-sickness has already been noted, as has the analogue between Louise and the courtly lady, all-important and yet neglected. Winterson further transforms the Petrarchan oxymoron of ice and fire for depicting the lover's plight, partly in imagery of winter and summer, but also through humorous transposition to secret love's gastronomical complement of awful meals passing from freezer to furnace (p. 72). Crucial is the recreated closet of self-sufficient isolation, created from within and without: inside, words change, honesty becoming "monstrous" the way "bauderye" becomes Troilus' "gentilesse" (*Troilus and Criseyde*, ll. III, 397, 402); a jealous world peers in from outside, correlative of an energy which cannot escape from lovers as self-sufficient and isolated as God, as their individual selves disintegrate to be completed in the other. Love's tragedy grows from a failure to acknowledge its "difference" which captures lovers in the scripts of illegitimacy.

Tradition clearly provides templets for this particular love story; but may also, as suggested above, serve Winterson more broadly, representing an epistemological stance that defines rationality and necessity within a framework of divine Love, a trope declaring "conceptual frameworks ... all and always provisional",[19] and requiring for its exploration analogues from human love and creativity: the cosmos dances for Winterson as for Dante. Turning the inquiry towards the human sphere, love and art are invoked to demarcate by their inassimilability the limits of cultural repetition, as verbal cliché, behavioral code, cognitive categories, and constructions of identity (psychological, sexual, social) dissolve under their risky play with necessity. Winterson's insistence that what

---

[17]   For further discussion of *Troilus*, Børch, *Chaucer's Poetics*, Bagsværd, 1993, chapters 5 - 9. Shakespeare's *Romeo & Juliet* may be said to represent this tradition, even as Dante constantly monitors his own love, notably in the Paolo and Francesca episode in *Inferno*, V.

[18]   The most famous critique of such readings is D.W. Robertson Jr.'s overreaction in e.g. "The Concept of Courtly Love as an Impediment to the Understanding of Medieval Texts" (1968), *Essays in Medieval Culture*, Princeton: Princeton University Press, 1980.

[19]   Winterson in *Gut Symmetries*, p. 168.

plays on the margins of discourse—the demonic-uncanny—has value, and validates the contingent as the source of its perception, counters postmodern strategies by which a similar recognition stops at exposing contingency's hollowness; and, consequently, challenges the postmodern pathos of disillusioned "ars moriendi"[20] with the comedy of "ars vivendi".

Love is the force that boxes clichés into new shapes. One turning-point in *Written*—when suddenly a chasm opens between the words and emotion of love—springs from one of the book's few "fantastic" moments. The lovers ascend by a spiral stairway to a towering place where children's voices mingle with those of tradition, embodied in Geoffrey Chaucer, one of the madmen who have struggled to transform the love that cannot be spoken into speech. The voices

> highpitched and eager, carried up past the sedater rooms and came at last, distorted, to our House of Fame. Perhaps we were in the roof of the world, where Chaucer had been with his eagle. Perhaps the rush and press of life ended here, the voices collected in the rafters, repeating themselves into redundancy. Energy cannot be lost only transformed; where do the words go?
> "Louise, I love you" (p. 52).

Where, indeed, do the words and the energy go? The lover's cliché betrays the emotion, since a "precise emotion needs a precise expression" (p. 10). *Written*, however, charts the process by which tradition helps bridge the chasm between cliché and precision, and is even renewed in the act: so, who did come first? And as for clichés, they *are* the problem; and yet as outbursts they harbour the motivational grain from which, to echo the misprised father himself,[21] new poetry sprouts in tradition's old fields.

---

[20] McHale (n. 13), p. 232.
[21] *Parliament of Fowls*, ll. 22 – 25; Winterson, *ArtOb*, p. 126: in "the new work, the past is [not] repudiated; quite the opposite, the past is reclaimed".

The Word Embodied in *Art & Lies*

by Cindie Aaen Maagaard

Art & Lies is one of Jeanette Winterson's most strange and lyrical novels, and one that adds itself to Winterson's constant experimentation with new ways to reflect artistically on the linguistic nature of human experience. Like all of her novels, *A&L* is concerned with the problem of how universalizing tendencies within discourses of identity, gender, love, sexuality, and belief determine—and often contradict—the complexities of life experienced by the singular subject. A novel of existential contemplation, *A&L* is also a moving consideration of the problem that our only recourse is to language that is never completely our own, but is rather a predetermined system that in turn determines us through a network of signs and symbols so "total that they bring to [man's] birth [...] the shape of his destiny".[1]

In *Art & Lies*, Winterson turns her critical imagination to the issues of ethics phrased in Handel's Socratic refrain, "How shall I live?", and shows how the question finds an echo in Sappho's lament over the dead Word. Thus, the novel becomes an examination of the role of the Word in the reflections, decisions, and desires which constitute ethical responses to the question of how one should live. How can one speak or write, or even think, about life, *A&L* asks, when "the world is a charnel house racked with the dead" who speak "the dried-out shrivelled-up babble of the morgue" (p. 64)? How can one love, when the sentence "I love

---

[1] Jacques Lacan, "Function and field of speech and language", in *Ecrits. A Selection*, translated by Alan Sheridan (London: Tavistock, 1977), p. 68.

you" is "the murder weapon of family life", in Picasso's experience (p. 154)? How can one reflect on one's own experience when one feels, like Handel, "dumb inside a borrowed language, captive of bastard thoughts" (p. 22)?

Or: how can we hold language accountable, when it is precisely when we speak and "[enter] the medium of language" that we relinquish the very singularity that is necessary in order to assume responsibility for our lifeview and commitments to others?[2]

Possible answers begin with the resurrection of the dead Word, which Winterson undertakes in the novel. In order to do this, she reaches back to the biblical Word and sends it into combat against the postmodern one—not in an effort to impose absolutes, but in order to imagine how the signifier can be made to answer to, and for, what it signifies. What emerges is an ethics of the Word that is closely tied to the erotics of the body; and both of them are motivated by desire that incites the intentional movement toward—and ultimately, responsibility to— the other. Along the way, Winterson plays with postmodern and premodern conceptions of textuality and materiality and their bearing upon the power of the Word to signify, envisioning in the dialogue between them language that is responsible for what it names, yet not tyrannic.

Winterson's consideration entails that she situate herself within the poles of postmodern attitudes toward language that arise in light of poststructuralist awareness of the perpetual play of signification and deferral of meaning described by Derrida's *différance*. If, on the one hand, we are liberated from considering language a means by which to pin down any one, definitive meaning, we have on the other grown suspicious of the slipperiness of language, the elusiveness of meaning, and any claim of language to apprehensible truth. Regardless of whether we view "play" affirmatively or skeptically,[3] philosophical cognizance of the textual nature of truth and the figural nature of language invariably influences and can conflict with what we feel to be ontological truths about our lives. That the distrust of language is potentially so disturbing discloses the degree to which we are dependent upon language to anchor us in the world and to each other, and the extent of our desire for language to refer to something other than itself, for signs to refer to something other than other signs. Derrida relates this to our human condition, defining "man" as "that being" constituted by a wistful desire for "full presence, the reassuring foundation, the origin and the end of play".[4] That

---

[2] Jacques Derrida, *The Gift of Death*, translated by David Wills (Chicago and London: University of Chicago Press, 1995), p. 60. Derrida discusses this question with relation to Kierkegaard's reading of the story of Abraham and Isaac in *Fear and Trembling*.

[3] For a discussion of these two views of postmodernity, see Pauline Marie Rosenau, "Affirmatives and Skeptics", in *The Fontana Postmodernism Reader*, ed. Walter Truett Anderson (London: Harper Collins, 1996), pp. 103 - 05.

[4] Jacques Derrida, *Writing and Difference*, translated by Alan Bass (Chicago: University of Chicago

presence, however, is an impossibility: not only because any sign, including the linguistic one, means by virtue of difference, but because experience itself is linguistic, a function of its iterability, which presumes its difference and differentiation from something which it is not.

The Fall from Edenic innocence offers an apt metaphor by which to conceptualize the poststructuralist critique of presence, as seen in the work of a number of critics.[5] From prior existence in a state of undifferentiated goodness, Adam and Eve attain the knowledge of differentiation itself: experience of evil and its difference from goodness, and herein apprehension of the very difference that makes signification possible. The passage from Adam and Eve's pure understanding of God to His subsequent withdrawal from the world requires that He reveal Himself through signs, and with this move, semiology is born.[6] As sign, God is no longer outside the system of signification that relies on, and structurally contains, difference, and thus, is no longer the transcendental signified by which unequivocal meaning can be guaranteed. The Fall, then, is metaphor for the unknowable origin of difference—a "story of proliferating dualisms", entailing that from "God's presence we pass to His absence; from immediacy to mediation; from the perfect congruence of the sign and referent to the gap between word and object" (Hart, p. 8). The harder the fall, the greater the gulf between signifier and signified, word and object, image and referent.

As the dualisms snowball down to postmodernity, the widening of the gap between sign and referent to abysmal distances characterises the fallen state of language, in which simulation has won out over substance, and, as Baudrillard puts it, signs of the real have come to substitute for the real itself.[7] This is the kind of language that threatens to turn "progress" into "one of those floating comparatives, so beloved of our friends in the marketplace", as Handel notes (*A&L*, p. 109). In other words, the sign, now at several removes from its referent, signifies only itself. It "bears no relation to reality", claims Baudrillard: "it is its own pure simulacrum" (Baudrillard, p. 170). Baudrillard, too, invokes God in order to explore the nature of signification, asking whether representations of divinity signify a supreme authority "incarnated in images as a visible theology" or whether the very icons and images, with their "power of fascination", are themselves substitutions for the divine (Baudrillard, p. 170). Where once the

---

Press, 1978), p. 292.

[5] Kevin Hart is one critic who offers a succinct and lucid discussion of this metaphor, in *The Trespass of the Sign* (Cambridge: Cambridge University Press, 1989), pp. 3 - 21. Hart's book, particularly Chapter 1, has helped form many of the ideas presented in this article.

[6] It is the origin of theology as semiology, according to Hart, p. 7.

[7] Jean Baudrillard, "Simulacra and Simulations", translated by Paul Foss, Paul Patton and Philip Beitchman, in *Jean Baudrillard. Selected Writings*, ed. Mark Poster (Oxford: Polity Press, 1988), p. 166.

premodern conception of the bondedness of sign and referent made idolatry possible as the worship of the visual image *as gods*, postmodern "play" with images and symbols now invites the worship of image *as image*.

The self-referring image is for Umberto Eco cause for an ironic distance to the Word, a postmodern—self-conscious—mode of using language that prompts the speaker or writer to voice, in varying degrees of explicitness, reservations about the words he or she employs, since the histories of repetitive usage with which they are laden cause countless displacements of meaning. As Eco explains, for a man to say "I love you madly" to a cultivated woman would call up a stack of Barbara Cartland novels that would undermine the authenticity of his feelings for her.[8] Therefore, the postmodernist must "play the game of irony" in order to avoid the kind of "false innocence" toward language that deludes her into thinking that she can speak or write originally and unambiguously. As Eco puts it, the postmodern ironist would put it, "As Barbara Cartland would put it, I love you madly" (Eco, p. 32). Thus, the postmodern ironist exposes, rather than conceals, the quotedness of language, which calls its legitimacy into question. Winterson's Sappho *can* play this game, employing ironic, invisible, quotation-mark capitals to complain about the Very Famous Men who have silenced her throughout history. She also evinces a critical distance to words of love that is similar to Eco's reservations: "I know it will not be enough to say I love you. I know you have heard it before", she says (*A&L*, p. 139). Yet for Sappho, irony is less a matter of learning to play games than an insistence that language must be revived—through poetry, imagination, authenticity of emotion—if it is to answer to individual experience.

An awareness of the constructedness of language pervades every aspect of the novel. "It isn't natural, language", Sappho knows (p. 138), just as Handel states, "language is artifice" (p. 184). In *A&L*, Winterson voices the postmodernist's dilemma: how to guard oneself against "false innocence" but at the same time believe strongly in language as a means of expressing and examining experience sufficiently to grapple with Handel's question. This struggle between suspicion and faith is played out rhetorically in the novel, in a tension between the postmodern Word (with all the skepticism and play it calls up) and attempts to use words to imagine the Word as substance, the prelapsarian Word of innocence, but not naiveté, that Winterson situates in the body. On the one hand, we are made aware of the disruptions between language and corporeality, and on the

---

[8] Umberto Eco, "Postscript to *The Name of the Rose*", in *The Fontana Postmodernism Reader*, ed. Walter Truett Anderson (London: Harper Collins, 1996), p. 32. The notion that "I love you is always a quotation" is also the very premise of Winterson's *Written on the Body*; for a discussion of how Winterson comes to grips with this problem in that novel, see Marianne Børch's article, "Love's Ontology and the Problem of Cliché", in this volume.

other, we are brought to imagine language that seeks toward unity, substance, and presence. Thus, the text becomes an experiment in closing, or at least bridging, divisions between Word and referent and spirit and body, in reassembling the broken pieces of human beings and society.

In their contemplations on society, belief, relationships, and art, Handel, Picasso, and Sappho each critically consider the incongruity between the Word and how its signification is felt, and often contradicted by, the body. Subjectivity *is* linguistic, yet even Freud asserts that "the ego is ultimately derived from bodily sensations, chiefly from those springing from the surface of the body".[9] Knowledge about the world and the self is *also* corporeal, coming to us through sensations of sight, sound, smell, and touch that both reveal and provoke feelings of pain, pleasure, desire, fulfilment, power, and vulnerability. As Edith Wyschogrod explains, glossing Condillac, the pressure of touch on the body enables it to "[register] ... everywhere along its surface the fact that it is a body" (Wyschogrod, p. 62). And, I would add, a unique body: physical sensation can never be reproduced, but only ever approximated, in an other. Moreover, words such as "pain" and "pleasure" are prime examples of the extreme subjectivity and undecidability of signification. Indeed, corporeal experiences are always unique to the individual—though they are neither unambiguous nor, as Wyschogrod points out, outside the system of signification that enables the body to be "read" (p. 62).

Each of the characters' loosely bound narratives not only speaks of distances between themselves and others, but is underwritten by an examination of how language facilitates them, of how the contemporary Word divides Word from body from spirit. For Handel, this is one cause of the fall from authenticity of emotion and purpose that makes his utterance, "still we long to feel" ring with poignancy and irony (p. 14). His passages test the rhetoric of his professions, which minister either to body or spirit, but never both simultaneously: both the priest's "homily on the Will of God" and the doctor's "baby language about [the] heart" come up short in the face of human suffering and death (p. 184). This is language removed from the corporeal realities it seeks to express, by which the medical profession can defend the removal of the wrong breast by "[calling] the botch a complication" (p. 123), and apply the imagery of the stage to the harsh reality of abortion: "The rule had been a success, few abortions were performed. Performed. Back stage things went on as usual, unrehearsed, unregulated, without proper equipment, but for a very good price" (p. 178).

Handel counts himself among the practitioners of sterile professional vocabularies that are impotent in the face of events of suffering, pain, and death.

---

[9] Cited in Edith Wyschogrod's inquiry into an ethics of the body, "Towards a Postmodern Ethics: Corporeality and Alterity", in *Ethics and Aesthetics: The Moral Turn in Postmodernism*, eds. Gerhard Hoffman and Alfred Hornung (Heidelberg, Universitätsverlag C. Winter, 1996), p. 64.

Because Handel's question constantly haunts him, as it reverberates through each line of daily small talk, he is compelled, as priest and physician, to heal himself. He undertakes a self-diagnosis of body and spirit which ache precisely because they are split through the intervention of language that can only speak through euphemism and cliché, voicing nothing. Yet Handel knows himself to be guilty of having resorted to the comfortable Word: "Honeyed words, hadn't he said them? The rational man with the musical voice, 'There's nothing to worry about. Nothing to fear, go on, get dressed'" (p. 126). His passages reveal that it is fear in the face of the other that diseases the human heart, a sickness facilitated by, and concealed within, the discourses that deny the truths the body tells us. And Handel's history speaks of that fear—his repeated withdrawals from spiritual and physical love into the self-protection of cool reserve.

Ultimately, language fails him. "What shall I call it?" he asks, struck dumb by a woman's "Beaver? No good. It looks nothing like a beaver or a pussy or a fox. Cunt? Is that the best I can do for those delicate labial folds and the monkish cowl that hides..., that hides..., a bead, a pip, an acorn, a pearl, a button, a pea..." (p. 18). Like Ruggiero, confronted with "a woman's ... a woman's ... what should he call it?" (p. 28), Handel experiences how the mystery of the body surpasses its epithets. "I'm supposed to have all the answers, aren't I?" he asks himself on his mother's death, but the overwhelming excess of meanings that constitutes the very singularity of death silences him. "A priest, a doctor, you'd expect me to be able to say something careful and comforting.... There is no answer, because there is no question" (p. 116). How to name what exceeds all capacity to be contained in human words? Handel's awe in his encounter with the body recalls the humility in the face of the divine that renders it impossible to signify God adequately. In his relation to the sacrality of the body, Handel recalls Augustine, who asks, "Have we spoken or announced anything worthy of God? Rather I feel that I have done nothing but wish to speak: if I have spoken, I have not said what I wished to say".[10] Handel wrestles with the implications of our inability to transcend the human language that determines us, as our imperfect system of signs means we speak about ourselves when we mean to speak about something other. In its failure, then, Handel's discourse is a kind of "negative theology" of the body, aware of its own impotence in the face of the overwhelming.

As in Handel's fragments, Winterson explores through Picasso's story the way in which language belies the truths that become known to us because they are felt on and by the body. The word in question in Picasso's fragments is "love", which has degenerated from cliché to bald-faced lie, as the signifier of physical

---

[10] Augustine, *On Christian doctrine*, translated by D. W. Robertson, Jr., introduction by Thomas Merton (New York: Library of Liberal Arts, 1958), Book I, vi (pp. 10 - 11). Cited by Hart, in a discussion of negative theology, p. 6.

and emotional tyranny practiced by the family. In Picasso's experience, "I love you" is "the murder weapon of family life", the "worn-out words, that when they are not blunt, are sharpened on a lying-stone. When do they pierce the skin?" she asks. "When they are true, or when they are false?" (p. 154). The truth of love is precisely that it is disclosed as untrue by what Picasso knows corporeally: the physical pain of rape, her body torn by her brother "as crows do lambs", and her father's attempt to murder her by pushing her off the roof, "the day and hour" of which are indelibly "written on her body" (p. 85). From her family, Picasso seeks salvation in color and light and the discomfiting art of the painterly vision which comprehends "the shock of the familiar, suddenly seen" (p. 90). Her struggle to defy mediocrity and pursue her art in accordance with her own creative impulses requires that she break with her family, who threaten to stifle her as an artist and murder her very being. To do so necessitates new ways of defining the word "love" outside "the sick semantics of family life" (p. 82).

It is in Sappho's fragments that the recovery of the Word on behalf of all three of the characters is attempted most boldly. Here, Winterson expands the possibilities that lie within the notion of body-as-text to be a means by which the chasm between Word and its referent not only is disclosed, but closed, as sign and substance become one. First, simply, Sappho is the Word embodied. She represents a literalization of the figurative expressions that conceive text as body and the body as text, as well as the fragmented nature of discursive identity in postmodernity. Sappho *is* the remnants of her poetry, but she is also a living woman. She confuses the ontological order of the world of the novel as she is read by the other characters within it, including Doll Sneerpiece (herself both a bawdy and a text read by the other characters), but also joins them as a living character, even falling in love with Picasso-Sophia. The Word incarnated in the figure of Sappho suggests a reimagining of the mechanisms of signification by transforming the metaphorical to the literal and conflating sign and the substance of its referent, as language itself becomes material, known as body and through it. While in *Written*, the body is a text to be read by the lover, in *Art & Lies*, body is not only text, but text is also body, or that which is capable of being sensed by it. This union of the intelligible and the sensible recurs throughout Sappho's fragments, as she sings the material Word: "the word and the kiss are one", "my words on yours forms words I do not know" (p. 66), "the word whose solace is salt from the rock", "the word shaped out of substance", "the word imposed upon substance", "the word out of flux and into form" (p. 55), "the word made out of fire and fire from the word" (p. 74).

Out of the mouth of the Greek poet also come allusions to the biblical Word of presence. She repeats the creative Word of Genesis, the *logos* by which God initiates being in the act of naming it, "the Word itself is day and the Word itself is night" (p. 55), and alludes to the New Testament *logos* of Christ's embodiment of God's word, represented by the ingestion of Christ through the Eucharist: "I cannot eat my words, but I do. I eat the substance, bread, and I take it into me, word and substance, substance and word, daily communion, blessed" (p. 55). As they are voiced by Sappho, the Old and New Testament Words become paradigmatic for the poet, who is herself a creator of worlds, and one who conceives the restoration of the Word as an act motivated by love. She alludes to Christ as God's gift of love, as the Word that "became flesh and made his dwelling among us" (John 1: 1- 14); this is the "Word in human form, Divine" which she invokes (*A&L*, p. 202), the same creative Word of love, poetry, and power that is summoned by writers through the ages to write the Book that is the metaphor of all books, which Handel reads at the end of the novel.

Through Christ, and through the sacrament of the Eucharist, God's love as presence is tangible, ingestible, givable, and receivable. Through Sappho,Winterson herself appeals to pure *presence* as a means to imagine the Word anchored in what it names, a signifier in perfect union with its signified. Winterson plays with a notion which imagines a limit to the play of difference. Hart's explication of the significance of Christ as sign illuminates the brilliance of Winterson's move: "Like other signs, Christ is both signifier and signified, body and soul. But Christ is also unlike other signs, for here the signified—God— is perfectly expressed in the signifier. He is at once inside and outside the sign system; since Christ is God, what he signifies is signified in and of itself" (Hart, p. 8). Thus Winterson reaches back to the Bible for a means to envision a cure for the postmodern Word separated from its object.

In similar images in the second of her sections, Sappho contemplates the relation of word to body to spirit. First, the Spirit is identified with "the ideas that form life", and constitutes the "images that outlive ... [the] flesh", yet her meditation mediates a passage between spirit and body: "Why split the soul from the body and then the soul from itself?" Finally, as she speaks to the absent Sophia, the body is conceived as words "revealing now, themselves" (pp. 143 - 44). Sappho's conception of the relation between soul, flesh, and text evolves from Platonic or Cartesian dualities of spirit and body to a union of them—in which the body is a text deciphered through touch, and the reading resuscitates language, releasing "the living word" (p. 144).

Although it requires a leap of imagination of the reader trying to grasp its possibilities, envisioning the Word embodied is more than an empty exercise in conceptualization. Rather, Winterson retrieves the premodern in order to experiment with the notion of a return to non-differentiation: what if the Word were what it names? What if it were bound to the body? What if the Word were a gift of love? It seems a risky game to play, but I do not mean to claim that Winterson desires to reinstate the language of totalities and absolutes, which seeks to obliterate difference. Rather, Biblical images of the material Word are a means to hold the sign accountable for what it names, in an ethics of the Word that is very much bound up with the erotics of the body.

Winterson's focus here is on how the Word becomes a bridge to the other, a means to actuate the subject's movement toward the other, motivated by the desire which arises out of the gap between other and self. The substantiation of the Word that is, or can be sensed by, the body is in the novel facilitated by, or itself facilitates, the turning of one being toward another in an act of love. For the poet Sappho, sex is a "lexigraphic fuck" between two lovers who body to body form a "couplet" (p. 74). Intercourse is penetration by the word, Sappho says: "The word inside me, I become it". The pleasurable mingling of bodies as words is a "re-virgining" of the fallen Word, a making new and whole (p. 74). In other images, the desire that moves the self toward the other recalls religious love, and the commission of the prophet. The Word enters Sappho through her mouth, in a lover's kiss, like the holy spirit—"Kiss me with the hollow of your mouth and I shall speak in tongues (p. 65)—and in a later passage, she is likened to the prophet into whose mouth God puts His Word: "The word ... puts a god in her mouth" (p. 73). The Word is associated with bread and wine, honey, love, sex, and spirit—appetite, pleasure, desire.

So, as it emerges in *Art & Lies*, Winterson's is an imaginative ethics that seeks out the possibilities for self-knowledge and understanding of the other, through language which arises out of, or stimulates, corporeal experience. But as always in Winterson, it is love that brings the subject into being. It is when Sappho receives the word from her lover's mouth that the dead word awakens, and in the following mysteriously poetic passage Sappho experiments with possible names for the lover's kiss—"caress or salute", "billiard balls that touch", "a drop of sealing wax"—and her body: "My mouth on yours forms words I do not know. Shall I call your nipples hautboys? Shall I hide myself in the ombre of your throat? The rosary I find between your legs has made a bedesman out of me" (p. 66). Language becomes a means to know the lover physically, and bodily sensations become a way to know language anew.

As Sappho's search for the lyrical language that can do justice to her lover demonstrates, to mingle Word and body enables human beings to grasp truths about themselves which are disguised by euphemism, platitude, and cliché, but about which the body cannot lie—the pain of illness, suffering, and death, the pleasure of love, and even, in Winterson's vision, the experience of God. As one and the same as the very bodily sensations that give rise to desire, material language reawakens the "dead desire" that Lacan describes "as a desire that cannot speak its right name" but perpetuates itself through metonymic displacements and metaphoric condensations of the signifier.[11] In Sappho's imaginings, language does not approximate, but *constitutes* the desire of the body, just as the material word *is* the embodiment of emotion, thought, and imagination. I do not read Winterson's return to the material Word as a nostalgia for the notion that we can know prediscursive truths, or as a hierarchical prioritizing of flesh over spirit. For that, her imagery is too equivocal and playful; and as we have seen, her images insist on the mingling of the two, rather than their division into dualisms. Instead, hers is a way of envisioning how the play of signification can *move* us, by speaking to, and through, the body, relieving postmodern suspicion toward the word at so many removes from the world that is its own simulacrum.

Yet it is precisely as a move *within* the postmodern that Winterson can appeal to language as presence without appealing to the very absolutes, or "false innocence" about language described by Eco, that the novel resists. Instead, the premodern becomes a means to subvert the postmodern, and vice versa: Winterson's images of the substantiated Word are themselves linguistic, figural ways of *imagining* presence, not creating it. To believe otherwise would be falsely innocent. But by imagining language as desire, as bound to the corporeal experiences that are unique to each subject, Winterson imagines a means to enter the medium of language without entirely relinquishing the singularity that is necessary in order for us to assume responsibility for ourselves and others. Thus Winterson posits an answer to Sappho's question, "How shall I know these lines are my own, and not a borrowed text?" (p. 139).

Winterson's conceptions of the Word able to move us reflect metatextually on the novel as an ethical utterance, and the power of literary language to confront existential concerns. *A&L* demonstrates that asking "How shall I live?" requires asking "How shall I speak?" or "How shall I write?"—or even "How shall I read?". It is not far from our wrestling with the textual puzzles of the novel to speculations about the discursivity of our own existence. Moreover, as we experience the disturbing breaches of logic and linear temporality in broken narratives that mirror fragmented lives, we are confronted with our own desires for synthesis and sense, the impulse to bind together the wounds, holes, and gaps in the text. As we read Sappho's complaint, for example, itself embedded in Winterson's novel of fragments, we are made aware that we are adding ourselves to a chain of readers piecing together not only Winterson's text, but through hers, Sappho's. Our reading must resist the strategies of the Very Famous Men who reduce Sappho to simplistic labels.

The novel continually frustrates attempts to gather meaning into a manageable totality, because it deconstructively resists the imposition of absolute

---

[11] This is Peter Brooks' explication, in *Reading for the Plot* (Cambridge, Mass.: Harvard University Press, 1984), p. 58

meanings. Thus, in its refusal to give in to totalizing urges, *A&L* provokes in the reader an unease that resembles that of the characters, as they struggle within their separate chapters to reach toward others and to assemble the pieces of themselves. "Myself", Handel says, "[t]he accumulation of parts; menus, concert programmes, blood-pressure charts, books read, conversations overheard, irrational fears, recurring dreams, love lost and found" (p. 187). His list continues, but at least part of our ability to understand him rests in our ability to recognize his sense of the disparateness of existence in our own impossible task of assembling the text into a coherent whole.

Art & Lies certainly does not deny the disjointedness of life, but the novel offers other ways of redeeming meaning than smoothing over the wounds. Winterson summons the Word, makes it tangible, and restores it to authenticity, demonstrating that a critical stance toward language need not be a cynical one, and that language can be the medium of love. As an answer to Handel's "How shall I live?", the novel itself is an argument that we must do so "by the Word": by the Word that stimulates unease or pleasure, awakens desire, moves human beings emotionally, enables them to grasp truths about their predicament, and facilitates their movement toward each other.

Language and Lies:
Jeanette Winterson's Experimental Modes of Narration
by Mette Bøm

When I started to write about the subject of this article, the experimental writings of Jeanette Winterson as exemplified in her novel *Art & Lies*, the image of a child in front of a house of cards came to mind. When a child is confronted with a construction such as a house of cards, she will immediately try to break it; to make it collapse, the way she will also ruin expensive chinaware, or assert her will so strongly as to fall foul of her friends. As the child grows older, however, she is taught that certain things in life have value and should remain intact, and she will rarely question the system or order which in reality has been forced upon her.

The historical persons or mythical figures whom we characterise as rebels are those who, in some way or other, have questioned or refused to acknowledge such externally imposed systems of conduct. They have dared to challenge and to deconstruct society's regulations, structures and rules. They have, like Winterson's heroine Picasso, chosen their own staircase and "left home to paint", to live with the colours of life (*A&L*, pp. 40 - 41).

Jeanette Winterson is a rebel with regard to literature. Obviously dissatisfied with the current schools of literature, Winterson experiments in all her writings with the idea of order. She plays with expectations, associations, context and form. In *A&L* she tampers with the house of cards which has every literary construction under its roof, be it representational or structural.

I shall try to explain how and why I see Jeanette Winterson aligning herself in *Art & Lies* with the experimental writing tradition.[1] One might argue that my aim is based on a paradox—the paradox of trying to define, structure and provide answers in response to that which itself poses questions inherently sceptical of order, as is the essence of experimentalist aesthetics. However, my idea will be to adopt Winterson's own strategy of prioritising the critique of language. That is, I will examine my subject for the purpose of revealing how it works and understanding what it has to say, rather than determining its identity within a specific generic or other formal category.

What is experimental literature? In *A Room of One's Own*, modernist and experimental writer Virginia Woolf comes close to a definition. In the portrait of her protagonist writer Mary Carmichael, Virginia Woolf writes: "first she broke the sentence, now she has broken the sequence".[2] By resisting the conventional linear quest narrative, the framework of the *Bildungsroman*,[3] and by introducing short, abrupt rhythms, disturbing the flow of her narrative, Virginia Woolf, in the person of her character Mary Carmichael, questions the entire foundation of the nineteenth-century novel. To Virginia Woolf, "breaking the sequence" meant breaking with the reader's expectations of a forward narrative drive, e.g. a quest structure. It meant writing a multi-vocal, impressionistic prose suggesting an uncensored mind flow (a stream of consciousness). It was to be antiauthoritarian and non-absolutist (i.e., generating no single and definable truth), and, first and foremost, it meant a playful juggling with genre, temporality and archetypal constructions.

Recurrent themes in Woolf's writings as well as in much fiction by modernist women writers are those of sexual identity, language and female representation. Many of Woolf's texts involve the re-writing of myths and folk-tales—a technique Woolf uses to deconstruct the "woman as other" gender pattern and to create new representations of female experience.[4] Woolf envisioned an experimental text capable both of deconstructing existing patriarchal structures

---

[1] In my historical analysis of women's experimental fiction, I will draw on my thesis *In Quest of a Feminine Expression - on women's experimental fiction*, submitted in the spring of 1997 to the English Department of the University of Copenhagen.

[2] Virginia Woolf, *A Room of One's Own* (London: Penguin, 1945), p. 81.

[3] A literary term which defines novels of either artistic (*Künstlerroman*) or personal development. In her novel *To the Lighthouse*, Virginia Woolf mixes the two genres in the portrait of Mrs. Ramsey as well as in that of the artist Lily Briscoe. Mrs. Ramsey's unspoken thoughts and contemplations make up her personal "*Bildung*". Woolf's utilisation of the stream-of-consciousness technique in these chapters came to mark her dissent from the Victorian writing tradition and adherence to the modernist way of writing.

[4] The term "woman as other" is frequently used in feminist criticism, especially during the 1960s politics of the other. It is used to describe the psychological and physical perception of woman as of another substance than man. The term has roots in the biblical story of Eve's creation in the Garden

from within, and of helping to establish women as serious artists; "she wrote as a woman, but as a woman who has forgotten that she is a woman, so that her pages were full of that curious sexual quality which comes only when sex is unconscious of itself" (Woolf, p. 92).[5]

That current form was always associated with patriarchy and masculinity implies, of course, that experimental fiction, with its serious attack on linear and almost didactically authoritative narrative forms, occupies a position outside the dominant structure, which again implies a female position. Therefore it was, and is, often aligned with the feminist project.[6] Still, my argument is that most experimental writers, including Woolf, then and now concern themselves primarily with exploding dominant forms, in the subversion of traditional modes of literary authorial conduct, before they will consider building a feminist doctrine. I do believe, though, that most female experimentalists have a political agenda. But it is not their primary concern, and thus I think it does them more harm than good to place an experimental writer in a "feminist" or "lesbian" box—as indeed has been the case with Jeanette Winterson. It opposes the experimentalist aesthetic to create new narrative structures, since new structures could suggest new truisms or new "houses of cards". To Virginia Woolf, a "woman's sentence" was ideally a sentence freed of gender speculation,[7] and to achieve the same emancipation of a "woman's sentence" is arguably the goal in *A&L*, where Winterson is careful to advance the issue of gender within the general context of deconstructing systems and truisms. Or as she says herself: "There is no system that has not another system concealed within it" (*A&L*, p. 6).

Between the picket lines of the cultural, political and aesthetic post-war revolution that took place during the 1920s, women writers began to articulate a new mode of expression which could give voice to women writers who had been silenced by patriarchy's pervasive and complex linguistic system.

of Eden, which has been the point of departure for many Freudian, Jungian and Lacanian theories of female sexuality/psychology.

[5] See *A Room of One's Own,* pp.77 - 78, 91 - 92, 100 - 103 for Virginia Woolf's ideals of women's writing. The historical fantasy *Orlando* (London: Penguin, 1928) is a fictional example of Woolf's techniques and ideals for women's writing.

[6] For a more detailed discussion of binary thinking in Western thought and the concepts of "violent hierarchies", see the French post-structuralist Jacques Derrida in *Writing and Difference* (Chicago: University of Chicago Press, 1987).

[7] "Even so, the very first sentence I would write here, I said, crossing over to the writing-table and taking up the page headed Women and Fiction, is that it is fatal for anyone who writes to think of their sex" (*A Room of One's Own*, p. 102). For a more elaborate discussion of feminism's relationship with the experimental writing tradition, see chapter 1.7 and pp. 87 - 88 of my thesis, *In Quest of a Feminine Expression - on women's experimental fiction*, or consult Toril Moi, *Sexual/ Textual Politics* (New York: Routledge, 1988).

In her study of feminist literature, *The Feminist Critique of Language*, Deborah Cameron perceives writing "not as an organic growth out of general linguistic capabilities, but a technology"[8]—a technology of language which constituted Western society's machinery of "truth" and to which, Cameron argues, women writers through the years were denied access in a variety of ways. Virginia Woolf and her female contemporaries were well aware that not only had this system largely excluded them from the literary playing field, it actually denied them access to every sphere of power, whether social, political or economic. They considered language their most effective weapon in their struggle for recognition. And the more innovative the text, the better.[9]

Another theorist of women's experimental fiction, Nancy Gray, agrees with Cameron and argues in *Language Unbound* that "women writers who wanted to write as themselves must find relationships to speaking that do not trap them in gendered accesses to language, art or agency".[10] Gray argues that the entire story-telling tradition of Western society "assumes an origin-telos pattern in which truth is to be revealed by event, reason or metaphor" (Gray, pp. 24 - 25). These events and metaphors are always, Gray argues, based on the assumption that man is human and woman his object and support. Recent feminist criticism has made it its business to reveal the processes of these "androcentric constructs", as Gray names them. Thus Gray agrees that language is the primary tool with which modernist women writers rebelled against, and gave impetus to the break-up of, patriarchy's established machinery of truth and rules.

If it is from the fount of language that the processes of female oppression spring, then many experimental writers will live with the paradoxical situation that without language female subjectivity does not exist, without language there are neither true nor false representations of female experience; thus language is absolutely essential to the project of changing women's position in the world. Women experimental writers therefore were—and still are—forced to fight fire with fire and use language in their struggle against the patriarchal linguistic system of oppression. Winterson illustrates this paradox with her character Sappho who returns to the world to re-write the story of her relationship with Sophia (Picasso), and to take revenge upon the "Very Famous Men" who "lied" about

---

[8] Deborah Cameron, *The Feminist Critique of Language* (New York: Routledge, 1990), p. 5.

[9] For a more elaborate discussion and theorizing of the modernist experimental writing tradition, women experimental writers, patriarchy and language, see Nancy Gray, *Language Unbound* (Chicago: University of Illinois Press, 1992) pp. 1 - 37, and Ellen G. Friedman and Miriam Fuchs, *Breaking the Sequence: Women's Experimental Fiction* (Princeton: Princeton University Press, 1989) pp. 4 - 42. And for a more general discussion of the highly diverse modernist writing tradition, see David Lodge, "The Language of Modernist Fiction: Metaphor and Metonymy", in *Modernism: A Guide to European Literature*, eds. Malcolm Bradbury and James McFarlaine (London: Penguin 1991).

[10] Nancy Gray, *Language Unbound* (Chicago University of Illinois Press, 1992), pp. 2 – 3.

her, censored and burnt her poems. Sappho's only weapon (like Winterson's herself) is the written word—the same weapon that oppressed her.

Women have traditionally been seen as "other" than the norm in all social, political, and intellectual contexts. Their writing therefore became the voice of "the other". During the period from the 1920s to around the 1970s, women writers took great pains not to repeat the reality created by male history and ideology, but rather to represent the world in their own way and voice. Women's writing involves a scepticism towards conventional narrative techniques as based in untenable assumptions about chronology, causality, space, and identity, which again leads to the exploding of forms—in other words, to experimentation with the literary medium itself.[11]

During the 1960s and 70s, this rebellion took on a new political turn with the style of *écriture féminine*, which promulgated the idea of formulating a female language (a body language) expressing the bodily experiences of women. Texts by writers as diverse as Anaïs Nin, Marguerite Duras, Erica Jong, Hélène Cixous, Joyce Carol-Oates, and Monique Wittig appeared on the literary scene. These writers were out to change the archetypal representations and images of women as "other", as dark, mysterious and hysterical. They did so by offering new sexually outspoken interpretations of women's lives and experiences, which could celebrate instead of condemn women's difference.

It is this long tradition of experimentation that I see Winterson belonging to. And, as is my argument here, not only does her writing show strong adherence to the techniques of modernists such as Virginia Woolf, it also embodies the techniques of *écriture féminine*. In *A&L* both these loyalties are strongly in evidence. To emphasise the woman artist's alienation from the world of systems confined within too narrowly rational limits, Winterson contrasts the sterile, pallid writing tradition of the society in which Picasso and Handel live with Sappho's long passages of *écriture féminine*:

> This is the nature of our sex: She opens her legs, I crawl inside her, red-hot. I crow inside her like a Chanticleer, red coxcomb on a red hill. She says, 'My little red cock, crow again,' and I do, with all my pulmonary power. I crow into the faint red-rising sun. I crow into the dew-wet world. I split her with the noise of it, she shatters under me, in a daybreak of content (*A&L*, p. 53).

---

[11] For a thorough account of the *écriture féminine*, see Elaine Marks and Isabelle de Courtivron, *New French Feminisms* (Massachusetts: The University of Massachusetts Press, 1980).

All of Sappho's chapters are filled with this kind of impressionistic, passionate and sexual vocabulary, spoken by a voice freed from the constraints of an only apparently civilised world of stunted eroticism and creativity, whilst itself freed to release and reshape the cultural energy of texts suppressed by that world. In this manner, Winterson succeeds in voicing the "muted" narrative—the voice of female desire and sexuality—which has been censored for ages.

> [J]ournalists and novelists would have me believe [that] to write
> without artifice is to write honestly. But language is artifice. The
> human being is artificial (*A&L*, p. 184).

I have argued that the modernist and early postmodern traditions, in particular the *écriture féminine*, share as a common goal the investigation of language and its representations. In *Art & Lies* this linguistic investigation is carried to its extreme. *A&L* admits no absolutes. Instead, it challenges its reader to redefine his/her own constructions and definitions of truth.

One of the principal goals of postmodern experimentation is probably to establish an interactive process between writer and reader—to reveal the subjectivity of truth and thereby make us reject our deeply ingrained urge to find universal truths validated in external (though actually self-projected) ones, and engage instead in the participatory process of fiction-making. Winterson uses intertextual references as a device to parody the realist narrative's notion of history as a source of truth and reason, and to build of the debris new and complex truths. Apart from the most obvious references to the painter Pablo Picasso, the poet Sappho, and the composer Händel (all highly innovative artists), intertextual references abound in *A&L*. Actually one can conceive of the entire novel as a jigsaw puzzle made up of intertextual references. Händel's chapters, for example, make repeated reference to holy scriptures, rewrite biblical stories and quote directly from the Bible (e.g. pp. 116, 119). Sappho's chapters likewise point to the works of Ovid, representative of a Classical tradition often and extensively evoked in the work, and the Picasso chapters refer to the paintings of, for instance, Leonardo Da Vinci (p. 91) and Van Gogh (p. 155). There are also references to Winterson's own works (for instance to *Written on the Body*, p. 81), and directly as well as indirectly to literary "masterpieces" such as the works of D.H. Lawrence (p.121), and Eliot's *Waste Land* (pp. 90, 107). The world of music is prominently represented, as a sample of text and score of *Der Rosenkavalier* offers the gloss for the tentative resolution of the plot at the end of the work. Far from suggesting elitarian name-dropping, these representatives of an official textual, pictorial and musical canon of Western Culture are enlisted along with fabrications, fragments, texts unfinished and finished, noble and vulgar (such as the highly erotic, exquisitely vulgar recollections of Doll Sneerpiece), as equal contestants for inclusion in the Book of Tradition, embodied in the volume shown in Handel's hands in the opening, and described towards the end, of the work.

Intertextuality is a device that the author can use to tell stories of both literature and history. But very importantly, it can establish a creative collaboration between author and reader. Winterson's intertextual references do both. They work to unmoor us from the security of what to expect from a book and engage us in a game of guessing, questioning and analysing the truths that our culture privileges in such books. Winterson plays with our urge to find a plot, a narrative pattern in the mosaic of images, voices and stories intertwined in the novel. A story may in fact be detected in that mosaic, but it has to be built through vigorous construction work on the part of the reader scrutinising, and herself scrutinised even in the act of scrutinising, the web and woof of Winterson's text.

"Question!" Winterson seems to shout at us when time and time again she imitates and rewrites the great masterpieces of the past. Suppose history is only a human construction made from un-authenticated scraps of paper, by a "baggy-trousered bus conductor" (pp. 52-53) and collected in "The entire and honest recollections of a bawd"? Where will that leave human knowledge and reason? How can Handel—a doctor—live and practice if he can no longer rely on the "clean white coats of science" for objectivity (p. 30)? Through referential play and imitation, Winterson channels authorial "responsibility" onto her reader in the hope that he or she will interpret and appreciate the novel as a writing of experience—truth in the making, as it were—and not a new set of truisms paraded as eternal and universal Truth.

Art & Lies thus constitutes what Catherine Belsey calls an "interrogative" text, in which no system or hierarchy will lead the reader to a truth validated in extratextual norms. The polyphony of the text has deprived the author of her authority, and the reader, Belsey writes, is left to "construct meaning out of the contradictory discourses which the text provides".[12]

"It could be that this record set before you now is a fiction" (p. 30), Handel says, leaving us to question the referentiality of the text, and thus Winterson's role as "author". By constantly drawing our attention to the fictitiousness of her own text, Winterson shows us how the author's role is to acknowledge and reveal the discursive nature of her own work and of reality by employing a self-reflecting, non-authoritative voice. To emphasise this idea, Winterson not only sets her own voices into play with tradition's voices, but also constantly repeats the truisms of modern-day culture—such as, for example, "a women who paints is like a man who weeps", "[a] woman cannot be a poet", and "single women become pregnant

---

[12] Catherine Belsey, *Critical Practice* (New York: Methuen, 1980), p. 129.

so that they can live off the State" (pp. 38, 52, 181)—and juxtaposes them with the personal experiences of her characters. Winterson's argument is that truisms are experienced as true only until they are challenged: as Picasso states, "lies are comforting, so long as they can be believed" (p. 43).

According to *Art & Lies* nothing in this world can be a universally and objectively true statement; "even science which prides itself on objectivity, depends on both testimony and memory" (p. 29), Handel says. All texts are fictions, reflecting one person's subjective selection of truths, which again means that nothing can be completely accounted for. Reality is a human construction as well, and as Nancy Gray notices, it "represents truth according to the motivations of the culture in which it occurs, not according to some universal repository of irreducible fact" (Gray, p. 85). Reality is like the market forces as understood by Handel: "[t]here is nothing a priori about market forces, nothing about the market that isn't a construction and that couldn't be deconstructed" (*A&L*, p. 103).

When truth and reality are both discursive, so are phenomena like history and gender. Winterson illustrates this claim by reviving the forgotten lesbian poet of antiquity, Sappho. "There is no such thing as autobiography there's only art and lies" (p. 69), Sappho states, while she haunts the streets of London like a ghost, ridiculing and mocking the writers and historians who have destroyed her poems, her life's work, and tried to "document" her life the way they wanted it. Truisms, Sappho says, only produce a collective, highly tendentious, version of history. Through the image of Sappho, then, Winterson reflects on the way male biographers and historians have created our history books—how our "objective" history and our perception of gender are merely collections of socially coded information and biassed impressions. Sappho shows us how male biographers have censored her story, i.e., the accounts of female experience that they did not find proper and did not want to hear—how history is indeed his(s)tory. She also shows how we, as readers, may piece Sappho together, too. It is no wonder, Winterson seems to say, that women have found themselves "other" than men, when they have only had the recollections of male biographers from which to patch together their own identities.[13]

Traditional culture has created a bleak and barren society, described by Picasso as a waste land of "rows of scuffed couches identically angled towards the identical televisions offering, courtesy of the bold white satellite dishes, forty-five different channels of football, news, comedy, melodrama and wildlife documentaries" (p. 83). A prefab "one size fits all"—world in which Picasso is a misfit, where she cannot breathe, live, speak (p. 155), or paint. It is an artificial

---

[13] In chapter two of *A Room of One's Own* Virginia Woolf makes the same point. Standing amongst thousands of books in the library, the narrator wonders why she cannot find any female history documented by women writers.

Brave New World scenario where a giant production machine pushes people "to and fro on invisible lines", and where all is accounted for and regulated by trains leaving at "5:45 to the suburbs" (p. 90).

This barren "Waste Land" is also echoed in Handel's chapters. Handel's world is a "terrible pantomime" where every mark of originality and difference is being wiped out by genetic engineers of his own profession (pp. 107, 112). People have shut their minds, deceived themselves about themselves, and have constructed protective shells to stop the expression of real emotion. In Picasso's case, this is vividly illustrated when she cannot give voice to her innermost fears and experiences. Her brother's sexual abuse of her is literally "put to sleep" in rooms that are "washed and decorated according to the latest fashion" (p. 43). Picasso is stashed away in a mental hospital and her mother wonders why she does not smile like "other little girls" (p. 85).

The human voice (the androgynous Sappho), creativity, colour and art (embodied in Picasso), and male sensitivity (embodied in Handel) cannot find expression through traditional narrative patterns, nor within any other system of thought, Winterson suggests. The task of the artist-writer must be therefore to create disorder, to do as Picasso does and paint herself "like a Buddha in gold leaf" or "soak herself in magenta dyes" (pp. 40, 47). The task of the female artist must be to create a noise[14] which pierces through the "master narrative" and disrupts convention by stirring up colours in a black-and-white world:

> Picasso painted. She painted herself out of the night and into the
> circle of the sun. The sun soaked up the darkness from her studio
> and left a sponge of light .... Without thinking, Picasso ran into the
> parlour, into the newspapers, into the best clothes and the dead air.
> She was painted from head to foot (pp. 47).

Winterson's point is clear: urban society's machinery of civilisation, its language and its modes of thought have created false identities, among these false gender constructions, have twisted the myths and stories that are part of our educational legacy, and have exploited not only natural resources, but also human beings, causing these to forget their bodies and their sense of self. As language constitutes power and power is inherent in the dominant order, one must change language in order to change the order.

As the "story" of *A&L* develops, one becomes increasingly aware of the

---

[14] In his lecture "Order and Disorder in Film and Fiction", the experimental writer Alain Robbe-Grillet describes the effect that an experimental text can have: "When a system is highly improbable and highly complex, it will no longer be perceived as a system, and the information theorists say that what is involved at that point is noise" (*Critical Inquiry*, Autumn, 1997), p. 8.

subordinate role of continuity of plot, and so of conventional notions of time, space, and character. Winterson's long lyrical passages of extravagant verbal and visual play, the proliferation of Sappho's thoughts and meditations, the constant shifts in time, generic play, changes in point of view, intertextual fireworks, and overlapping of contradictory historical data—all these point forward to a rejection of the "past" as previously, and traditionally, constructed; superseding it is that past reconstructed in the "now", i.e. as a truth filtered out of the data of life and organised into a pragmatically useful past. The real action, then, the action of identity-formation, takes place in between the mind-flow of the characters.

Like any other writer, Winterson shows herself critical towards one-dimensionality, hierarchy and regimentation. As a self-critical writer in line with the postmodern rejection of totalising systems, Winterson feels it her duty not to promote any structure to the status of another "master narrative", or produce new authoritative systems of thought, but instead to dismantle existing systems and question even the constructions she herself has created as narrator. That is why Handel repeats his truisms again and again[15] and why many of Handel's statements are constructed with an implicit question, an interpretation and deconstruction:

> 'How are you Handel?'
> (How shall I live?)
> 'What are you doing these days?'
> (How shall I live?)
> 'Heard about the merger?'
> (How shall I live?)" (p. 25)

Winterson deconstructs all habitual responses within her stories: Handel is asked a question which he himself questions (in the parenthesis); and within every story told in the novel, there is another story told from a different point of view, by a different character. Picasso's "suicide", for example, is told from Picasso's own point of view on pp. 44 - 45 and again on p. 158: "As it happened I did not fall on my own. As I stood slightly swaying, completely unafraid, my father pushed me off the roof". Then the "suicide" is told by Sappho, and later interpreted by Handel. To Winterson there is no core, no "master narrative", no objectively truthful account of events. Therefore, Winterson at the end places her characters—the outcasts, the doubters and the non-believers—on a train "travelling steadily towards the sun" (p. 15). Detached from the artificial world or the "dark carriage", as Handel calls his life, each character can at least leave behind a useless, lie-entrammeled past and open him- or herself to a real self under the auspices of

---

[15] See *A&L*, pp. 13, 27, 28, 98, and 109.

art; to an identity fluid, but dynamic and creative, and one that strengthens the fragile ties that tie each protagonist to the other two. It is not the "story" Winterson wants us to focus on, then, but the processes of mental change that each character undergoes, as he or she leaves the established order and, emancipated, enters into the world of fiction, art and creativity. "Things fall apart, the center cannot hold", Yeats wrote; in Winterson's words this becomes: "No-one has been to the very bottom. Except by inference we do not know that there is a very bottom. We do not know it from observation" (*A&L*, p. 32). Still, her characters find that they need not know the bottom to exist, and even live.

In this manner Winterson rewrites the traditional quest-narrative (with its more material objectives) into a quest-narrative for the exploration of love and identity. Sappho's, Picasso's and Handel's quests are inner searches for consciousness, for love—quests to analyse and to eventually eliminate their own false constructions and falsified notions of gender, social standing, and religion. But the quest for a self is an ongoing process. Winterson's message is for the reader to do like Picasso, Handel and to some extent Sappho; to board the train, reject a burdensome past, and reconstruct it in accordance with a valuable life in the "now". There is time for nothing else. As Picasso expresses it: "I've been unfortunate, it's true, hard-hurt and despised. But should I tell that tale to every passer-by? Should I make my unhappiness into a placard and spend the years left decorating it? There is so little time" (*A&L*, p. 92).

The place of experimental fiction in our literary tradition has proved to be more than a temporary fling. But creative innovation and rebellion are short-lived and soon become part of a tradition. Therefore, I believe one should try to understand the currents of this innovative literary venture before it assimilates into another "order" and norm.

But why is it important to investigate this?

Because the work of the contemporary generation of female experimentalists, such as Jeanette Winterson, Barbara Guest, Kathy Acker, Luisa Valenzuela, Christine Brooke-Rose, Joyce Carol Oates, Monique Wittig, and Angela Carter, sheds new light on the nature of language, life and contemporary female experience. Instead of rejecting those who try to change our perspective on life by calling it diffuse, confusing and abnormal, as indeed has been the label pinned on much experimental fiction, including some of Jeanette Winterson's work, I believe we should try to examine and interrogate the rebels of literature in the same manner that they seek to question our perception of life. We should follow the example of Picasso, who "shied away from what she couldn't understand, and, at first, disliked those colours, lines, arrangements, that challenged what she thought she knew, what she thought to be true", but then learned to love what was experimental and discomfiting. In other words, we must keep investigating the texts until they make sense to us—until they become events, rather than "objects fixed by time" (*A&L*, p. 39).

Upon encountering Winterson's highly innovative writing techniques, even the inexperienced reader will discover the powerful way language works as the primary constitutive factor in human thought. Therefore she will understand how important it is for those seeking to understand life constantly to question, expose and criticise the representations that language produces.

> I like to look at how people work together when they are put into stressful situations, when life stops being cosy, when it stops being predictable, when there is a chance element which unsettles all the rules, which forces people back onto their own resources, and away form their habits. Always in my books I like to throw in that rogue element into a stable situation and then see what happens.[16]

In the experimental writings of Jeanette Winterson, there is a rebellious spirit, an urge to transform language and thereby the established structures and conventions of modern society. I find it interesting to witness how Winterson questions and challenges her reader's perception of truth and reality by discussing taboos, by rewriting myths (such as the myth of Sappho and Sophia), by overturning and systematically deconstructing conventional notions of truth, authority and representation, and by treating time and space in an unorthodox manner. Breaking, deconstructing and shattering language, narrative structures, time, plot, and voice—all this, I realise, makes the immediate message of *A&L* sound pessimistic. But however self-doubting and disillusioned the characters of the novel may seem, it becomes increasingly clear that Winterson's view of language is not pessimistic at all. Winterson does succeed in telling her stories of Handel, Picasso and Sappho. She does succeed in reminding us of the dangers of a monolithic view of the world, of structures, rules and regulations, and of the demolition of difference created through oppression or exclusion, whether motivated by biasses about religion, race, gender, or social status. So Winterson does believe in taking an active part in discourse and in wielding the powers of this discourse. But she does it to insist that language constructs multiple realities, none of which should be allowed to suppress any other, and that to understand the current state of female experience we must constantly scrutinise discourse by eliminating the constructions of difference which uphold oppression. I find Winterson's attitude absolutely necessary to the world of literature and art. And absolutely vital to any process of change.

---

[16] Jeanette Winterson in an interview with *Salon Magazine*, April 97. From www.salonmagazine.com.

Like the work of Sisyphus, the task of experimental fiction is never-ending, since literature as a reflection of life and society constantly creates new constructions of reality. As long as there is fiction, there will be new representations to challenge. Or, as Jeanette Winterson says herself in an interview with *Salon Magazine*, "[a]ll of my books end on an ambiguous note because nothing ever is that neatly tied up, there is always another beginning, there is always the blank page after the one that has writing on it. And that is the page I want to leave to the reader".[17]

---

[17] Ibid.

"Shadows, signs, wonders":
Paracelsus, Synchronicity and the New Age of *Gut Symmetries*
by David Lloyd Sinkinson

> Now, more than ever, crossing into the twenty-first century, our
> place in the universe and the place of the universe in us, is proving
> to be one of active relationship (*Gut Symmetries,* pp. 97 - 98).

As a work of fiction, *Gut Symmetries* is open to all types of interpretation with its allusions to the Tarot and Kabbalah, and its mythical, astrological and alchemical references.[1] The temptation is to head straight for a dictionary of symbolism and begin to discern a number of interesting patterns throughout the text. Critical responses to the book have, however, been mixed. Helena Grice and Tim Woods, studying the "dislocated discourses" of the novel, believe that it "ultimately produces a narrative which falls apart rather than falls together".[2] Similarly, Katy Emck in her review sums up the book as a "beautiful, stirring and brilliant story,

---

[1] One interesting reading is to make an astrological study of the three main characters based on the time and place of their birth. I asked an astrologer friend, who has not read the book, to describe the characters based on their charts. Significantly, Jove turned out to be dominating, proud and lacking in any contact with his feelings, whereas Alice has a deep need to seek a higher order in the universe and Stella has a desire for uninhibited self-realization. (My thanks to Christina Sanchez for her research.)

The quotation "shadows, signs, wonders" is from *Gut Symmetries*, p. 89.

[2] Helena Grice and Tim Woods, eds., *"I'm telling you stories": Jeanette Winterson and the Politics of Reading* (Amsterdam and Atlanta: Rodopi, 1998), p. 118.

but it does not really make sense".[3] What Emck is trying to make *sense* of here is the relationship between the main characters: "Although the novel takes the love triangle as its theme, it is hard to care what happens to Alice, Stella and Jove" (Emck, p. 21).

I do not wish in this paper to attempt to help "make sense" of the work as a whole, so much as to point out two features which may suggest how to read a story which is "a journey through the thinking gut" (*Gut Symmetries*, p. 13). These are the presence of Paracelsus in the prologue and the role of coincidence in the dramatic birth of Stella (*GutS*, pp. 83 - 94). In my discussion I will also make reference to Winterson's own comments about art and language as she puts them forth in *Art Objects*.

Gut Symmetries opens with the birth of the sixteenth-century Swiss physician and alchemist, Paracelsus, who wrote in such a way that his statements could be accepted as neither true nor false; his writings were neither strictly logical nor illogical but were to be read with an open mind to his mystical prose. This is a congenial paradigm for Winterson's own exploratory fiction. Paracelsus serves as a call for a new way to describe the universe, and this is reflected in Winterson's innovative portrayal of events, in particular her exceptional attentiveness to the concept of time. Indeed, she seems to have her finger on the pulse of a way of experiencing events in time which places her in the spirit of the New Age. This is displayed by the way *Gut Symmetries* introduces a little gem of a word, *synchronicity*, caught in the net of a bracket (*GutS*, p. 120), after virtually thirty years of floating around in areas as diverse as psychoanalysis, popular New Age books and recently, films and pop music.[4]

Carl Jung has defined the concept of synchronicity as "the simultaneous occurrence of two meaningfully but not causally connected events".[5] An observer of a meaningful coincidence may say that some principle of fate or destiny is involved. But Jung rejects any deterministic system, preferring instead to study the non-causal correspondences between the inner world of the unconscious and

---

[3] Katy Emck, "On the High Seas of Romance", *Times Literary Supplement*, 3 Jan. 1998, p. 21.

[4] For an introduction to the concept, see Allen Combs and Mark Holland, *Synchronicity* (New York, Paragon House, 1990). Also, Arthur Koestler, *The Roots of Coincidence* (London, Picador, 1974), especially chapter 3. I believe the first use of the word in a film is Mike Leigh's *Career Girls* (1994), and it is the title of an album issued in 1983 by the pop group, The Police. The lyrics also capture the new scientific spirit: "Effect without cause / sub-atomic laws, scientific pause / Synchronicity". Winterson is not the first novelist to use the word. It appeared in Paul Auster's *Moon Palace* (1989). The concept is not isolated and has relatives in other literary concepts, such as André Breton's notion of *le hasard objectif* and a more distant cousin, in Horace Walpole's *serendipity*. No doubt other comparisons can be found.

[5] Carl C. Jung, Synchronicity: An Acausal Connecting Principle (Princeton, N.J.: Princeton University Press, 1973), cited in Carolin S. Keutzer, "The Power of Meaning: From Quantum Mechanics to Synchronicity", *Journal of Humanistic Psychology,* 24 (1984), pp. 80 – 94.

the outer world of "reality". What is so intriguing about Winterson's sensitivity to the role of time in *Gut Symmetries* is the focus on the precise timing of conception (Alice's father will not make love to her mother until he has been promoted) and the birthdates of her characters, which not only have astrological significance, but as we shall see in the case of Stella, celebrate the act of creation.

> Nov 10 1493. Einsiedeln, Switzerland. Birth of Paracelsus.
> Nov 10 1893. Einsiedeln, Switzerland. Rebirth of Paracelsus.

Jung celebrated the four-hundredth anniversary of the alchemist by giving two lectures on him and reading him as a Jungian—or was it Paracelsus being understood for the first time? Jung needed, like the poet-character Stella, to find the "inner life, the other language" of the world within (*GutS*, p. 45). Paracelsus is introduced in the prologue of the novel to represent the intimacy of the inner world with the outer: "Paracelsus was a student of Correspondences: 'As above, so below.' The zodiac in the sky is imprinted in the body. 'The galàxa goes through the belly.'" (*GutS*, p. 2).[6] For Jung, Paracelsus and Winterson, this intimacy between the self and the world is not part of an astrological determinism but a creative relationship based on the power of the imagination. Paracelsus expresses this in the following way in *De Virtute Imaginativa*: "Man is a star. Even as he imagines himself to be, such he is. He is what he imagines ... Man is the sun and a moon and a heaven filled with stars ... Imagination is Creative Power". [7] This special relationship between ourselves and the world means that language is continually creating the world anew. As Winterson asserts: "The artist is a translator, one who has learned how to pass into her own language the languages gathered from stones, from birds, from dreams, from the body, from the material world, from the invisible world, from sex, from death, from love" (*ArtOb*, p. 146). The language "gathered from stones" represents the type of thinking common to both Paracelsus and Winterson.

One of the many languages Winterson utilizes is that of the new physics to describe the relationship between the self and others. Winterson lights up a multifarious firework of scientific analogies to describe the relationships in the book.[8] For example, Alice depicts Jove as "unstable as uranium. Stella, a living fission" (*GutS*, p. 198). Her affair with Jove is presented in alchemical terms:

---

[6] Cindie Maagaard explores the close bond between word and body in her article "The Word Embodied in *Art & Lies*" in this volume.

[7] Paracelsus, from *De Virtute Imaginativa*, cited in *Encyclopaedia Brittanica, Macropædia*, William Benton, 1974, volume 13, p. 983.

[8] Compare Goethe's use of one simple scientific analogy of *de attractionibus electivis* to represent the relationships of characters in his novel *Elective Affinities* (London: Penguin, 1971).

"Our affair, like every other, was conducted inside a vas hermeticum: a sealed vessel, shut off from the world, to boil and cool according to its own laws" (*GutS*, p. 100). Alice considers whether the continual heating of their bodies to absurd temperatures of a "billion degrees K" to a "quadrillion degrees" would finally bring them together.[9] Winterson draws on scientific language to explore love because no one true representative language of love has ever been written.[10]

Winterson invokes Paracelsus as an artist-scientist, working from the gut and partaking in the creation of reality in the process. As she remarks in *Art Objects*: "The earth is not flat and neither is reality. Reality is continuous, multiple, simultaneous, complex, abundant and partly invisible. The imagination alone can fathom this and it reveals its fathomings through art" (*ArtOb*, p. 151). Similarly, in *Gut Symmetries*, Alice is seeking a reality in which she can find Stella and must acknowledge that in such a search "(t)he universe is a rebus" (*GutS*, p. 206). The rebus, a symbol here of the emblematic riddle of the universe, is to be discovered *non verbis sed rebus*: not in words but through things. Winterson continually places the world of things into our bodies: "Your open mouth spewed up the Thames" (*GutS*, p. 210). This is the "universe opening in your gut" (p. 2). Throughout *Gut Symmetries* there are references by Stella to the world inside herself: "What I see, what I touch is interior, either I am inside it or it is inside me" (*GutS*, p. 47). The universe inside ourselves. The microcosm within. This Hermetic model of a world within is reflected by the birth of Paracelsus at the opening of the book: "First there is the forest and inside the forest the clearing and inside the clearing the cabin and inside the cabin the mother and inside the mother the child and inside the child the mountain" (*GutS*, p. 1).

The world is contracted into the womb of the mother and within the womb is the mountain of the world. Why should Winterson be so interested in the birth of her characters and their search for their parents? *Gut Symmetries* hinges on the fact that the universe begins with us and we begin with the universe—*with birth at a unique moment in time.* The embodiment of the universe being created within ourselves is a major theme in *Gut Symmetries* and for Winterson a clue to understanding the nature of the universe. But what is nature? Winterson herself answers this question in *Art Objects* by taking the etymology of the word: "From the Latin *Natura,* it is my birth, my characteristics, my condition" (*ArtOb*, p. 150). Winterson then goes on to list the properties of nature and ends with the statement, "[a]nd not just myself, every self and the Self of the world" (*ArtOb*, p. 150), as if the world is a living organism within herself, a continually regenerating *natura naturans* within her gut. The role of the mother and father in the birth of

---

[9] The use of the Kelvin temperature scale hints at the name of Paracelsus, *para* - Celsius, to move beyond traditional measurements.

[10] On this see Marianne Børch's article, "Love's Ontology" in this volume.

the three main characters Stella, Alice and Jove is of fundamental importance to the story because the meeting of the parents and their love is the story of the birth of—and the story of—the characters themselves.

Reading Carl Jung's lectures on Paracelsus, Winterson would have been struck by the emphasis Jung placed in the role of the mother for the alchemist's thinking, so that the whole world of the sixteenth century thinker

> assumes maternal form, from the Alma Mater of the university to the personification of cities, countries, sciences, and ideals. When Paracelsus says that the mother of the child is the planet and the star, this is in the highest degree true of himself (Jung, p. 112).

The maternal world of Paracelsus comes to represent the world within ourselves. The mother, child and star are depicted in the novel by the diamond swallowed by Stella's mother, centred in the base of the spine of Stella (Latin, *stella*, "star") and with its connotation of sparkling light, the diamond is the star of Stella.[11] Let us take a closer look at how birth is depicted in *Gut Symmetries*.

Winterson pays meticulous attention to the exact timing of the births of her main characters and this precise recording, in terms of date, place and astrological position, is not simply to make the reader aware of the uniqueness of birth. It has more to do with a sense of connectedness, of a cosmic *symmetry*. We are part of a curved universe: "If light travelled in a curved line it would mean that space itself is curved. / (Pitch of her body under me.) / 'Alice?'" (*GutS*, p. 17). The consequence of a curved universe here is that the narrative can include interjections from other worlds. Winterson is not only teasingly bending the Euclidean love triangle to adapt it to a lesbian relationship but also incorporating the fourth dimension of time. Who is interrupting the flow of Alice's story with the unidentified "Alice?" Is it Stella responding to Alice's contemplation of her body? Alice reiterates this intimacy of the curved universe and the female body reflecting on Stella: [12] "Is that her breast under me? Sphere of the thinking universe, wilful plunge of the sea?" (*GutS*, p. 19). The typographical curved lines of the

---

[11] Stella's birth is explicitly linked to the Hermetic notion of the microcosm-macrocosm: "On the night I was born the sky was punched with stars. Diamonds deep in the earth's crust. Diamonds deep in the stellar wall. As above, so below" (*GutS*, p. 187). In the prologue to the book, a baby is defined as a "culet", which is the smallest surface on a cut gemstone (*GutS*, p. 7).

[12] It is as if by stressing curvature, Winterson transforms the use of Luce Irigaray's use of the medical *speculum* (i.e. a curved mirror) of the female body and transforms it into the speculum of her own telescoped universe within, the "magic mirror" of the alchemists (*GutS*, p. 12) in contrast to the numerous references to plane mirrors in the book: e.g. Alice's "hall of mirrors" (p. 12) and Stella's "I looked in the mirror. Was that my face?" (p. 34). See Margaret Whitford, ed., *The Irigaray Reader*, Basil Blackwell, Oxford, p. 6.

parentheses represent Alice's reaction to Einsteins's theory of relativity, that "the shortest distance between two points is a curve" (*GutS*, p. 17). We do not meet these curved lines again until the introduction of the concept *synchronicity*.[13] The use of parentheses in Alice's meditation on Stella is appropriate because it suggests the closeness of two separate beings. Parenthesis: from the Greek *parentithenai*, literally, "to put alongside": a symmetry or coincidence of two dissimilar elements within a text.

The passage in which synchronicity is referred to occurs as Alice reflects upon her meeting with Stella and Jove, her own past and her father. Alice the scientist is reflecting upon the possibility of a special connection between events:

> In space-time there is always a lag between prediction and response (synchronicity is a higher dimension phenomenon where the rules space-time do not apply), sometimes of seconds, sometimes of years but we programme events far more than we like to think (*GutS,* p. 120).

Alice is suggesting here that life's progression is not just a series of random causes and effects but is influenced by the human psyche, which shapes a "programme of events". For example, without Alice's initial affair with Jove, Stella would never have met Alice. "How strange", Alice repeats to herself (*GutS,* p. 16) like Alice in *Alice in Wonderland*, thinking about the events leading up to her meeting with Jove, god of fate.

Stella's own birth is similarly part of an extraordinary occurence of events but in her case the events happen simultaneously. She is called forth by her own father. But in this case it is not a birth simply *caused* by his calling. It is an episode of a "higher dimension", without cause or reason, *concurrent* with the calling. Naming and creation are one. Here is Paracelsus' idea that imagination is a creative power. It is with the seemingly coincidental timing of his calling out the name of Raphael (the angel) and the rescue of Stella's mother by Raphael (the Polish immigrant) that we can describe the event as synchronistic. The mother is of course sceptical:

> That Papa with his shawl, his boxes, his stones, his books, his mutterings, his sleepless years, could pierce events and alter them,

---

[13] Einstein, whose birth is also marked (*GutS*, p. 23), was the inspiration for Jung's new concept. "It was Einstein who first started me off thinking about a possible relationship of time as well as space, and their psychic conditionality. More than thirty years later this stimulus led to . . . my thesis of psychic synchronicity" (Jung, cited in Roderick Main, ed., *Jung on Synchronicity and the Paranormal*, London, Routledge, 1997, p. 16).

that was not science. Not common sense. She *thanked chance and Raphael*, and only once did she look at Papa as though she might, perhaps, believe him (*GutS*, p. 92, my italics).

Here the mother reads the event as mere chance; but to have faith, and believe in the "language gathered from stones" of Paracelsus, would require one to accept that the sign of Raphael is that of the angel, even though this may contradict traditional science and common sense. There is a simple yet eloquent remark made by Alice near the beginning of the novel about the way we reach out to love and the uncanny way we meet our future lovers: "The probability of separate worlds meeting is very small. The lure of it is immense. We send starships. We fall in love" (*GutS*, p. 25).[14] There is a suggestion here that basic human desire is a way of connecting: a *gut symmetry*. This connective impulse is the "affect of vision", the unconscious "programme of events" or rather, an affect of creation in the sense of making new connections in the world. Stella notes that the Hebrew "to know" in the Torah is "not about facts but about connections" (*GutS*, pp. 82 - 3). If the universe is contained in our gut, in the centre of ourselves, then so are all our close relations. One Jungian psychoanalyst has emphasized this: "In the experience of a synchronistic event, instead of feeling ourselves to be separated and isolated entities in a vast world we feel the connection to others and the universe at a deep and meaningful level".[15]

Through the character of Stella's father, Winterson opens up a new way of perceiving, although it should be noted that the act of naming takes place within the fathers's own Jewish mystical tradition: Stella is called forth from the deep gut feeling of her father, who calls "from the Creation" and "with the voice of the prophets" to create his daughter (*GutS*, p. 90 - 91). And as a calling, Stella's birth is the start of a journey: significantly, both Stella and Alice are born in the tiny space of a moving vehicle represented by a sleigh and a tug respectively. But for Winterson they also evoke an "alchemic vessel", a microcosmic world of "a finite enclosure of floating space, a model of the world in little" (*GutS*, p. 9) floating upon the macrocosmic waters of mother earth.

The influence of "other worlds" and the symmetry of parallel universes are reflected in the Tarot images which link each chapter. The birth of Stella is

---

[14] A potential theme in the attraction of the two opposites—Stella the poet and Alice the scientist—has a parallel in the poem *Paracelsus* by Robert Browning, of Paracelsus the scientist and Aprile the poet: "*Paracelsus:* Die not Aprile! We must never part. / Are we not halves of one dissevered world, / Whom this *strange chance* unites once more?" (my italics). (Browning, *Paracelsus*, II, 587 - 589, in *The Poems of Browning*, eds. John Woolford and Daniel Karlin, [London: Longman, 1991], pp. 187 - 188.) Interestingly, love is "like a chance-sown plant" (ibid, V, 686, p. 300).

[15] Jean Bolen, *Tao of Psychology: Synchronicity and the Self* (New York, Harper & Row, 1979), p. 24.

represented iconographically by the Star Tarot card. The card shows a naked woman kneeling by a stream, pouring water from two pitchers. She represents the goddess of the regenerative waters and thus a form of rebirth. In this way a meta-narrative is built up out of the correspondence consisting of the river (as time flowing) related to the birth of Stella in the frozen water of the snow. A Jungian, writing about the woman in the Star Tarot card, refers to this intersection of the temporal and eternal realms: "She appears at the point where the living water of the collective unconscious touches the earth of individual human reality".[16] When the collective unconscious is activated, there is a potential for a synchronistic event: the vertical element of eternity touching the horizontal plane of the temporal text. The reader is prepared for the supra-human character of Raphael's special powers when he is described as having "remembered a time before he was born, before his father was born, when someone who was still in his blood had travelled over the ice plains and the stilled rivers to fill a sledge with firs" (*GutS*, p. 85). The "stilled rivers" of time represent the eternal unknown self, the "someone" still in our blood, represented by the generations that went before. And thus Stella is called out "from the Creation" (*GutS*, p. 91) and the long line of the Jewish patriarchs by her own father, just as Alice is called by the forefathers of science: "Paracelsus, Jung, Einstein, Freud, Capra, and although I still know nothing, I am no longer a disciple of Fate" (*GutS*, p. 120).

The Tarot chapter-images help to invoke a sense of "other worlds" which suggest archetypal images outside the ordinary flow of the narration. In this way we may not only read at the level of the story but on an archetypal level: Raphael, with his "Angel Car" (*GutS*, p. 85), is both mortal and angel, in the same way that the Jewish guide Azarius in *The Book of Tobit* (from the Old Testament Apocrypha) reveals himself to be the angel Raphael in disguise. In the offices of the Church, the ancient hymns composed for the feast of Raphael invoke the angel as the physician "*nostrae salutis medicus*": his name means "God has healed".[17]

To Winterson personally, this notion of a synchronistic experience is not unfamiliar. In an interview following the completion of *Gut Symmetries*, Winterson makes an allusion to these accidents of creation when talking about her own research, which took place during her reading of Jung.

I like to crawl around secondhand bookshops, and indeed libraries, and just see what's there. So there's that part of it that is haphazard. Except strangely enough, when I am about to write a book, I

---

[16] Sallie Nichols, *Jung and Tarot: An Archetypal Journey* (New York: Samuel Weiser, 1980), p. 295.

[17] E. H. Gombrich, *Symbolic Images* (London: Phaidon, 1972), p. 27.

always find exactly what I want by chance, it's one of those synchroncities.[18]

Out of the "haphazard" form of creation arise new combinations. Stella's mother is attracted to her husband "because he made vast systems out of nothing" (*GutS*, p. 80). Stella emphasizes the creation from out of creation, the *natura naturans* of her birth by mentioning that it occurs in the same year as the exhibition of Action painting in New York by Jackson Pollock, whose work was inspired by the ritual acts of artistic creation by native American Indians.[19] Although the process of having a hand in creation is not a new one for artists or scientists, it had revolutionary consequences when it was also found to apply to the discoveries of the new physicists in the twentieth century.

The idea that reality is not an autonomous phenomenon, but totally dependent upon the observer, acquired scientific respectability with Einstein's theory of relativity and Heisenberg's uncertainty principle.[20] These scientific theories created a tremendous release for Modernist artists in the early part of the twentieth century.[21] It is highly significant in this respect that Winterson's essays in *Art Objects* revolve around the period when both Modernist art and science experienced a fundamental break with conventional views of the representation of reality. An art object was no longer the reflection of an optically perceived reality but an aesthetically conceived recreation, where the perception of the artist was just as valid a reality as that of another viewer, which takes us back to the centrality of the imagination for Paracelsus.[22] As Winterson notes in *Gut Symmetries*, "Observer and observed are part of the same process. What did

[18] Winterson, interview in "Jeanette Winterson: The Art of Fiction", *Paris Review*, 145, Winter, 1997 - 98, p. 83.

[19] Pollock's own genesis is in turn referred to in the appellation of "that strange Wyoming-born Pollock" (*GutS*, p. 123). The capital of Wyoming, Cheyenne, is also the name given to a North American Indian tribe and its language, belonging to the Algonquian family. The affair between Stella and Alice is born in the Algonquin Hotel and with it comes a new language of love.

[20] Winterson is careful to explain this. Stella's father is an acquaintance of Heisenberg and the uncertainty principle is described by Stella. "When Heisenberg told him that every object can be understood as a point (finite, bounded, specific) and as a wave function (spreading infinitely though concentrated at different rates), Papa wanted to discover whether or not he could move himself along his own wave function, at will, whilst alive in his body" (*GutS*, p. 168).

[21] See Cyril Barrett, "Revolutions in the visual arts" in *The Context of English Literature 1900 - 1930*, ed. Michael Bell, (London: Methuen, 1980), pp. 218 - 240, especially pp. 238 - 240 on the standpoint of the scientific observer.

[22] No longer can we say that a "cat is a cat is a cat" (*GutS*, p. 81). This echoes Gertrude Stein's famous "A rose is a rose is a rose". Winterson is reflecting the paradigmatic shift in science in the twenties with the parallel revolution in the arts and at the same time breaking the old clichés to create a new language.

Paracelsus say? 'The galaxa goes through the belly'" (*GutS*, p. 162).

The narrative of *Gut Symmetries* is not then to be read for the traditional coherence of plot, as some critics believe, but rather for the sympathetic symmetries between characters: for some unknown reason, Stella's mother is drawn to Rossetti's diner owned by Jove's mother. "We think Mama was heading there on the night she gave birth" (*GutS*, p. 89). And further back in time, the brass plaques of Alice's grandmother are already shining from Liverpool to the harbour of New York (*GutS*, p.52). The birth of Stella is also celebrated at the end of the novel, with the neon face of Times Square (its lights created by the same man who had attended the viewing of Stella's diamond), which reveals "November 10 19:47", coincidentally the date of Stella's birth in 1947 (*GutS*, p. 219). These precise dates and their astrological implications serve to underscore the mysterious bond which is sometimes made conscious between people and events by the experience of a synchronistic experience.

We are not presented with the traditional facilitating of a plot. Winterson finds plots "meaningless" (*ArtOb*, p. 170) and this is reflected in her work and in her perception of the universe. As she states in *Art Objects*: "It may well be that nothing solid actually exists, but what might exist is energy, is space. And I have not discovered a more energetic space than art" (*ArtOb*, p.169).

I have been suggesting that synchronicity plays an important role in the birth of Stella. If we are to accept this, it also means that the universe, being within us, takes time to realize in terms of the creative process. It is a question of timing. But more than that: simply waiting. The birth of Stella is the mystery of the creative process itself and it is a symbol of Winterson's own intimate relationship with the word.

> The moment will arrive, always it does, it can be predicted but it cannot be demanded. I do not think of this as inspiration. I think of it as readiness ... For me, the fragments of the image I seek are *stellar*, they beguile me, as stars do ... but I cannot possess them, they are too far away. (*ArtOb*, p.169, italics mine).

I have limited this study to a single episode of the birth of Stella to show that through her interest in time, Winterson has applied Jung's concept of synchronicity to suggest how conception and birth are meaningful, rather than random, events in the creation of a universe continually creating itself. Winterson utilizes Paracelsus because his vision maintained an intimate relation between the word and the world and he acts as an icon to represent Winterson's continuing quest for a new (poetic-scientific) language to conceptualize and so make accessible the universe within us. But we should remember that this is a lyrical journey undertaken by three voices and their pasts. And like a diamond, the work should be rotated and viewed from different angles for its poetic symmetries to be fully appreciated.

Bibliography

Allen, Carolyn. *Following Djuna: Women Lovers and the Erotics of Loss*. Bloomington: Indiana University Press, 1996.

Anderson, Linda, ed. *Plotting Change: Contemporary Women's Fiction*. London: Edward Arnold, 1990.

Asensio, María del Mar. "Subversion of Sexual Identity in Jeanette Winterson's *The Passion*". In *Gender, I-deology: Essays on Theory, Fiction and Film*. Eds. Chantal Cornut Gentille D'Arcy and Jose Angel García Landa. Amsterdam and Atlanta: Rodopi, 1996, pp. 265 – 79.

Augustine. *On Christian doctrine*. Translated by D. W. Robertson, Jr. Introduction by Thomas Merton. New York: Library of Liberal Arts, 1958.

Barrett, Cyril. "Revolutions in the visual arts". In *The Context of English Literature 1900 – 1930*. Ed. Michael Bell. London: Methuen, 1980, pp. 218 – 240.

Barthes, Roland. "The Death of the Author". In *Image Music Text*. Selected and translated by Stephen Heath. London: Fontana Press, 1977, pp. 142 - 148.

Baudrillard, Jean. "Simulacra and Simulations". Translated by Paul Foss, Paul Patton and Philip Beitchman. In *Jean Baudrillard. Selected Writings*. Ed. Mark Poster. Oxford: Polity Press, 1988.

Beer, Gillian. *The Romance*. London: Methuen, 1970.

Bell, Michael, ed. *The Context of English Literature 1900 – 1930*. London: Methuen, 1980.

Belsey, Catherine. *Critical Practice*. New York: Methuen, 1980.

Bilger, Audrey. "Jeanette Winterson: The Art of Fiction". *Paris Review*, 145 (1997 – 98 / Winter), pp. 69 - 112.

Blake, William. *Jerusalem*. In *Blake: Complete Writings with Variant Readings*. Ed. George Keynes. London: Oxford University Press, 1996.

Bloom, Harold, ed. *Lesbian and Bisexual Women Writers*. Philadelphia: Chelsea House Publishers, 1997.

Bloom, Harold. *The Anxiety of Influence*. Oxford: Oxford University Press, 1973/ 1997.

Bolen, Jean. *Tao of Psychology: Synchronicity and the Self*. New York: Harper and Row, 1979.

Braidotti, Rosi. *Patterns of Dissonance. A Study of Women in Contemporary Philosophy*. Translated by Elizabeth Guild. (1st ed. 1991). Oxford: Polity Press, 1996.

Braidotti, Rosi. *Nomadic Subjects. Embodiment and Sexual Difference in Contemporary Feminist Theory*. New York: Columbia University Press, 1994.

Browning, Robert. *Paracelsus*. In *The Poems of Browning*. Eds. John Woolford and Daniel Karlin. London: Longman, 1991, pp. 187 – 188.

Brooks, Peter. *Reading for the Plot*. Cambridge, Mass.: Harvard University Press, 1984.

Bush, Catherine. "Jeanette Winterson: Why is the Measure of Love Loss?". *Bomb* (1993 / Spring), pp. 55 - 58.

Butler, Judith. *Gender Trouble: Feminism and the Subversion of Identity*. New York and London: Routledge, 1990.

Børch, Marianne. "Jeanette Winterson". *ANGLOfiles*, 100 (Feb. 1997), pp. 56 - 61.

Børch, Marianne. *Chaucer's Poetics: Seeing and Asking*. Bagsværd, 1993.

Chaucer, Geoffrey. *The Riverside Chaucer*. Ed. Larry Benson. London: Oxford University Press, 1988.

Combs, Allen and Mark Holland. *Synchronicity*. New York: Paragon House, 1990.

Currie, Mark. *Postmodern Narrative Theory*. London: Macmillan Press, 1998.

Curti, Lidia. *Female Stories, Female Bodies: Narrative, Identity and Representation*. London: Macmillan Press, 1998.

Derrida, Jacques. *The Gift of Death*. Translated by David Wills. Chicago and London: University of Chicago Press, 1995.

Derrida, Jacques. *Writing and Difference*. Translated by Alan Bass. Chicago: University of Chicago Press, 1978.

Derrida, Jacques. *Of Grammatology*. Translated by Gayatri Chakravorty Spivak. Baltimore and London: The Johns Hopkins University Press, 1976.

Doan, Laura. "Jeanette Winterson's Sexing the Postmodern". In *The LesbianPostmodern*. Ed. Laura Doan. New York: Columbia University Press, 1994, pp. 138 - 55.

Dumm, Thomas L. *Michel Foucault and the Politics of Freedom*. Thousand Oaks, London and New Delhi: Sage Publications, 1996.

Duncker, Patricia. "Jeanette Winterson and the Aftermath of Feminism". In *'I'm telling you stories': Jeanette Winterson and the Politics of Reading*. Eds. Helena Grice and Tim Woods. Amsterdam and Atlanta: Rodopi, 1998, pp. 79 – 88.

Eco, Umberto. "Postscript to *The Name of the Rose*". In *The Fontana Postmodernism Reader*. Ed. Walter Truett Anderson. London: Harper Collins, 1996, pp. 31 – 33.

Emck, Katy. "On the High Seas of Romance". *Times Literary Supplement*. 3 Jan. 1998, p. 21.

Faderman, Lillian. "What Is Lesbian Literature? Forming a Historical Canon". In *Professions of Desire: Lesbian and Gay Studies in Literature*. Eds. George Haggerty and Bonnie Zimmerman. New York: Modern Language Association of America, 1995.

Friedman, Ellen G. and Miriam Fuchs, eds. *Breaking the Sequence: Women's Experimental Fiction*. Princeton: Princeton University Press, 1989.

Foucault, Michel. "Nietzsche, Genealogy, History". (1st ed. 1971). In *The Foucault Reader*. Ed. Paul Rabinow. London: Penguin, 1991, pp. 76 - 100.

Foucault, Michel. *Power/Knowledge: Selected Interviews and Other Writings 1972 - 1977*. (1st ed. 1972). Translated by Colin Gordon, et al. Ed. C. Gordon. New York: Pantheon Books, 1980.

Foucault, Michel. *The History of Sexuality. Volume One: An Introduction*. (1st ed. 1976). Translated by Robert Hurley. London: Penguin Books, 1990.

Frye, Northrop. *The Secular Scripture*. Cambridge, Mass.: Harvard University Press, 1979.

Frye, Northrop. *The Great Code*. London: Routledge and Kegan Paul, 1981.

Goethe, Johann Wolfgang. *Elective Affinities*. London, Penguin, 1971.

Gombrich, E.H. *Symbolic Images*. London: Phaidon, 1972.

Grice, Helena and Tim Woods. *'I'm telling you stories': Jeanette Winterson and the Politics of Reading*. Amsterdam and Atlanta, Rodopi, 1998.

Groz, Elizabeth and Elspeth Probyn, eds. *Sexy Bodies: The Strange Carnalities of Feminism*. London: Routledge, 1995.

Haggerty, George E. and Bonnie Zimmerman, eds. *Professions of Desire: Lesbian and Gay Studies in Literature*. New York: Modern Language Association of America, 1995.

Hansson, Heidi. *Romance Revisited: Postmodern Romances and the Tradition*. Umeå University, 1998.

Hart, Kevin. *The Trespass of the Sign*. Cambridge: Cambridge University Press, 1989.

Hauge, Hans. "The Ethical Demand: Responding to J. Hillis Miller's 'The Roar on the Other Side of Silence: Otherness in *Middlemarch*'". *Edda* (1995), pp. 247 - 255.

Held, James. *A Dream of Essence: Permutations of the Self in Contemporary Fiction*. Ph.D. dissertation, Temple University, 1995.

Hinds, Hilary. "*Oranges Are Not the Only Fruit*: Reaching Audiences Other Lesbian Texts Cannot Reach". In *The New Lesbian Criticism: Literary and Cultural Readings*. Ed. Sally Munt. Hempel Hampstead: Harvester Wheatsheaf, 1992, pp. 153 - 73.

Hrushovski, Benjamin. "Fictionality and frames of reference: remarks on a theoretical framework". *Poetics Today*, 5 (1984 / 2), pp. 227 – 251.

Hutcheon, Linda. *The Politics of Postmodernism*. London and New York: Routledge, 1989.

Jung, C. G. *Paracelsus as a Spiritual Phenomenon in Alchemical Studies*. Routledge and Kegan Paul, 1968.

Jung, C. G. *Synchronicity: An Acausal Principle*. Princeton, N.J.: Princeton University Press, 1973.

Kauer, Ute. "Narration and Gender: The Role of the First-Person Narrator in Written on the Body". In '*I'm telling you stories': Jeanette Winterson and the Politics of Reading*. Eds. Helena Grice and Tim Woods. Amsterdam and Atlanta: Rodopi, 1998, pp. 41 - 52

Kermode, Frank. *The Sense of an Ending*. Oxford: Oxford University Press, 1968.

Keutzer, Carolin S. "The Power of Meaning: From Quantum Mechanics to Synchronicity". *Journal of Humanistic Psychology*, 24 (1984), pp. 80 - 94.

Koestler, Arthur. *The Roots of Coincidence*. London: Picador, 1974.

Kutzer, M. Daphne. "The Cartography of Passion: Cixous, Wittig and Winterson". In *Re-Naming the Landscape*. Eds. Jürgen Kleist and Bruce Butterfield. New York: Peter Lang, 1994, pp. 113 – 145.

Lacan, Jacques. "Function and field of speech and language". In *Ecrits. A Selection*. Translated by Alan Sheridan. London: Tavistock, 1977, pp. 30 - 113.

Lodge, David. "The Language of Modernist Fiction: Metaphor and Metonymy". In *Modernism: A Guide to European Literature*. Eds. Malcom Bradbury and James McFarlaine. London: Penguin, 1991.

Main, Roderick, ed. *Jung on Synchronicity and the Paranormal*. London: Routledge, 1997.

Marks, Elaine and Isabelle de Courtivron. *New French Feminisms*. Massachusetts: The University of Massachusetts Press, 1980.

McHale, Brian. *Postmodernist Fiction*. London: Routledge, 1987.

Moore, Lisa. "Teledildonics: Virtual Lesbians in the Fiction of Jeanette Winterson". *Sexy Bodies: The Strange Carnalities of Feminism*. London: Routledge, 1995, pp. 104 - 127.

Munt, Sally. Introduction. *The New Lesbian Criticism: Literary and Cultural Readings*. Hempel Hampstead: Harvester Wheatsheaf, 1992, pp. xi – xxi.

Nichols, Sallie. *Jung and Tarot: An Archetypal Journey*. New York: Samuel Weiser, 1980.

Onega, Susana. "*The Passion*: Jeanette Winterson's Uncanny Mirror of Ink". Miscelánea (Zaragoza), 14 (1993), pp. 113 – 129.

Palmer, Paulina. "Contemporary Lesbian Feminist Fiction: Texts for Everywoman". In *Plotting Change: Contemporary Women's Fiction*.

Ed. Linda Anderson. London: Edward Arnold, 1990, pp. 43 - 62.

Palmer, Paulina. *"The Passion*: Storytelling, Fantasy, Desire". In *'I'm telling you stories': Jeanette Winterson and the Politics of Reading*. Eds. Helena Grice and Tim Woods. Amsterdam and Atlanta: Rodopi, 1998, pp. 103 – 116.

Pearce, Lynne. "Written on Tablets of Stone?: Roland Barthes, Jeanette Winterson and the Discourse of Romatic Love". In *Volcanoes and Pearl Divers: Essays in Lesbian Feminist Studies*. Ed. S. Raitt. London: Onlywoman Press, 1995, pp. 147 – 168.

Pearce, Lynne. *Reading Dialogics*. London: Edward Arnold, 1994.

Pykett, Lyn. "A New Way with Words?: Jeanette Winterson's Post-Modernism". In *'I'm telling you stories': Jeanette Winterson and the Politics of Reading*. Eds. Helena Grice and Tim Woods. Amsterdam and Atlanta: Rodopi, 1998, pp. 53 – 60.

Raitt, S., ed. *Volcanoes and Pearl Divers: Essays in Lesbian Feminist Studies*. London: Onlywoman Press, 1995.

Robertson Jr., D.W. "The Concept of Courtly Love as an Impediment to the Understanding of Medieval Texts". (First printed 1968). *Essays in Medieval Culture*. Princeton: Princeton University Press, 1980.

Robbe-Grillet, Alain. "Order and Disorder in Film and Fiction". *Critical Inquiry*, (1997 / Autumn).

Rosenau, Pauline Marie. "Affirmatives and Skeptics". In *The Fontana Postmodernism Reader*. Ed. Walter Truett Anderson. London: Harper Collins, 1996.

Seaboyer, Judith. "Second Death in Venice: Romanticism and the Compulsion to Repeat in Jeanette Winterson's *The Passion*". *Contemporary Literature* XXXVIII (1997 / 3), pp. 483 – 510.

Shakespeare, William. *The Winter's Tale*. Ed. Ernest Schanzer. London: Penguin, 1969/ 1996.

Shumway, Suzanne Rosenthal. "The Chronotope of the Asylum: *Jane Eyre*, Feminism, and Bakhtinian Theory". In *A Dialogue of Voices: Feminist Literary Theory and Bakhtin*. Minneapolis and London: University of Minnesota Press, 1994, pp. 152 – 170.

Stowers, Cath. "The Erupting Lesbian Body: Reading *Written on the Body* as a Lesbian Text". In *'I'm telling you stories': Jeanette Winterson and the Politics of Reading*. Eds. Helena Grice and Tim Woods. Amsterdam and Atlanta: Rodopi, 1998, pp. 89 – 101.

Vice, Sue. *Introducing Bakhtin*. Manchester: Manchester University Press, 1997.

Waugh, Patricia. *Harvest of the Sixties*. Oxford: Oxford University Press, 1995.

Whitford, Margaret, ed. *The Irigaray Reader*. Oxford: Basil Blackwell,

Winterson, Jeanette. *The World and Other Places*. London: Jonathan Cape, 1998.

Winterson, Jeanette. *Gut Symmetries*. London: Granta, 1997.

Winterson, Jeanette. *Art Objects*. (1st ed. 1995). London: Vintage, 1996.

Winterson, Jeanette. *Art & Lies*. (1st ed. 1994). London: Vintage, 1995.

Winterson, Jeanette. *Written on the Body*. (1st ed. 1992). London: Vintage, 1996.

Winterson, Jeanette. *Sexing the Cherry*. (1st ed. 1989). London: Vintage, 1990.

Winterson, Jeanette. *The Passion*. (1st ed. 1987). London: Vintage, 1996.

Winterson, Jeanette. *Boating for Beginners*. (1st ed. 1985). London: Minerva, 1990.

Winterson, Jeanette. *Oranges Are Not the Only Fruit*. (1st ed. 1985). London: Vintage, 1990.

Woolf, Virginia. *Orlando*. London: Penguin, 1928.

Woolf, Virginia. *A Room of One's Own*. London: Penguin, 1945.

Worthington, Kim L. *Self as Narrative*. Oxford: Clarendon Press, 1996.

Wyschogrod, Edith. "Towards a Postmodern Ethics: Corporeality and Alterity". In *Ethics and Aesthetics: The Moral Turn in Postmodernism*. Eds. Gerhard Hoffman and Alfred Hornung. Heidelberg, Universitätsverlag C. Winter, 1996.

Index